n

Dry Gulch Outlaws

Link Bonner leaves Emma Fitzgerald behind in Fort Union when he gets word that one of the six Carp brothers, who raped and murdered his young Pawnee bride Yana, is on his way to Yuma. It took a year to find the first and youngest. Now three others are found and cut down without mercy, two more are in the Yuma area. Link drives stagecoaches out of Yuma for income while he pursues information about the outlaws. Emma has followed his trail and now intends to march straight into his heart, without barriers or nonsense from him. Reluctant at first, he grows fond of her, and begins to feel love. But he must finish what he started. Only Spike Carp remains with his gang of cutthroat Mexican bandits, and Spike intends to repeat with Emma what he and his brothers did to Yana. Emma and Link face the remaining killers together.

Dry Gulch Outlaws

George Snyder

A Black Horse Western

ROBERT HALE

© George Snyder 2018
First published in Great Britain 2018

ISBN 978-0-7198-2622-1

The Crowood Press
The Stable Block
Crowood Lane
Ramsbury
Marlborough
Wiltshire SN8 2HR

www.bhwesterns.com

Robert Hale is an imprint
of The Crowood Press

Typeset by
Derek Doyle & Associates, Shaw Heath
Printed and bound in Great Britain by
CPI Group (UK) Ltd, Croydon, CR0 4YY

*For the woman in the theater lobby who smiled –
a perfect Emma*

ONE

The buckskin stallion stood saddled in the corral, the bedroll tied down. Link put his boot in the stirrup, and when he swung up, the buckskin jerked a short buck.

'Hup,' he said. 'Hup, stop that.' He sat heavily in the Mexican saddle and wiggled for comfort, reins in hand. 'We both been too lazy.' He gently heeled in. 'Let's get to it. Them outlaws ain't going to sit and wait for us.'

That was the thing when a man wrapped himself around a woman. She wriggled under the skin and kept her presence known. After a time, she thought he couldn't get along without her. She had him. Link's heart had dried up like a tumbleweed two years ago, leaving his chest hollow as a drum. While he enjoyed the widow's company, he could walk away without a backward look or thought. He carried no feelings inside except vengeance.

Two days before, Emma Fitzgerald had told him she'd overheard Spike Carp asking around about the tall, Texas gent with hair the color of chestnuts, down to his shoulders, and eyes she knew as champagne, a pale, golden brown – a gray, Plains Stetson low over those eyes – Carp saying the gent dressed cowboy, as if he'd been a drover or rancher once. He wore his Colt Peacemaker with the holster leg-tied below his right hip.

7

No showdown happened because Carp quickly rode on. Emma told him nothing and the fort officers were not friendly. Link had once been an Indian scout – one of them, and none would speak against him to a stranger. The word was, Carp had ridden on down around Tucson or Yuma.

What Carp did not say was that two years before, he and his five outlaw brothers had dry-gulched a prairie wagon coming down from Wyoming Territory to settle in the southwest. Nor did he say how he and his brothers had held the couple for three days, each having many turns with the young, beautiful, Pawnee woman before they cut off her hair to make watch fobs, then shot her through the back of the head, then sliced off her breasts for tobacco pouches. And they didn't care that Yana was the wife of a former army scout and three months pregnant. Link had been shot three times and left on the prairie for dead. A band of Cheyenne had found him and gave him life again.

Link did not believe that he could ever care for anyone again. Two years ago, he had cared for the Pawnee princess, too young for him – nineteen to his thirty-nine – now she was gone – taking with her any happiness or enjoyment for life he'd felt. It had taken almost a year to find the youngest Carp – Roby, just seventeen; heavily influenced by his brothers, especially the oldest, Spike. Link had found the boy a hundred miles out of San Antonio, camped next to eight rustled Texas longhorns with two other young outlaws.

He gunned down the two jaspers. He hung Roby, screaming and jerking by his heels from a sycamore, naked, and with the boy's own hunting knife, gutted him and his innards bounced in his young face when the wind blew the branches.

The act carried a message to the other five Carp brothers.

They came for him while he went after them – Link, not caring who found whom first, or what order he killed them. The hunt became difficult when the brothers had a falling out and argued then split. Link had wanted to kill them all together – now he would have to seek them out one at a time.

Cookie Carp was the middle brother at twenty-four. Link found him in the Dakotas stealing gold from small-time prospectors. Cookie was a loner, seldom mixed with other folks, and fancied himself a quick-draw gunfighter. Link busted into his camp and shot him in the knee. With a lariat around the outlaw's ankles, Link had dragged him at a fast trot and gallop, along a rocky creek for most of the next afternoon. That had been last summer.

Now, riding outside Fort Union, New Mexico Territory, east of the Rockies, Link twisted to look back. Parting with Emma Fitzgerald, the cavalry-officer widow who was just past thirty, had gone well enough – as good as those things went. They held each other, her body tight against his, their lips melted together while she vowed she would follow wherever he went. He liked holding her tight. Some men might have called her too skinny. He wouldn't. Women worried too much over losing their weight, afraid they'd get too thin to attract a man.

Beyond the fort, he hunched his back against a chill, northern wind that blew down from Canada, his Stetson low over his eyes. It felt pleasant to ride in the open again. Fort smells of burning firewood, cooking meat, outhouses and animal leavings, gave way to the scent of brush and grass, and rain clouds, pregnant and heavy. Early winter days were crisp though dirty clouds continued to bunch overhead.

The land was mostly flat, the prairie covered in buffalo grass dotted with balls of mesquite and juniper, but also with sections of rolling green and jagged hills which he camped within at night. On the third day, small herds of buffalo grazed in clusters around him as he kept the buckskin at a slow walk – groups of twenty or so, hump-backed with big, bent, woolly heads showing stubby horns. A bunch of five raised their eyes enough to stare at him as he passed fifty yards away, their jaws working on grass. Their scent reached him too. The buckskin walked easy, quiet and docile, turning his head on occasion to shake it at the herds. Link swallowed from his canteen and squinted along the horizon.

He reckoned to keep south to San Miguel, then ride across the wagon route that lay east to Fort Smith, Arkansas – staying along the Gallinas River, the prairie to his left.

Two days later, a few miles east of the river when crossing the open range, he saw a group of six Indians on a knoll, barely within sight. Too far to tell what they were, likely Cherokee or Choctaw – no painted faces. They and their mounts stared at him, a single rider crossing the prairie. They moved to the edge of the knoll but stopped without coming down.

Link reined the buckskin still. He swung down from the creaking saddle and lifted the stirrup to hook the horn. The buckskin turned his head and touched Link's shoulder. Link pushed into his slicker. He tightened the cinch then paused. At the knoll, the mounted Indians had not moved. The stirrup fell and he stared at his deerskin gloves against the side of the saddle.

An image of Yana came to him, angry with him, standing with her hands on her hips, lips tight, squinting at him, her sweet face working to show him she was not pleased. What it was that set her off he couldn't remember. He had stood close in front of her, looking down at that face. He had lightly kissed her forehead, eased around behind her and kissed the back of her black hair, moved further and kissed her ear, then come forward and kissed her nose. She relaxed and pounded his chest with her small fists, but not too hard. He had made her smile.

Sometimes memories crawled back inside as a reminder. As if he needed reminders. He stood still long enough for the buckskin to turn his head toward him again.

He stepped up into the saddle. 'You be ready to run,' he said, and leaned over and patted the buckskin on the side of the neck. 'Be set to go when you feel my urge.' He gently heeled the horse off again.

The Indians remained on the knoll.

Link passed, still seeing them above the horizon, unmoving. When he had gone by, and they were fading from view behind him, he glanced back and saw them ease over the edge of the knoll and come down to the prairie. He heeled the buckskin to an easy gallop.

The first, heavy, drops of rain splatted against his Stetson and slicker. Immediately, it poured heavily.

The Indians jumped to a full gallop after him.

Link heeled the buckskin to run. He pulled the Henry and held it in the crook of his arm. The first rifle shot snapped through the air, but he didn't see where the slug went. He glanced back. The six were spreading out in a line, sitting high, riding fast, rifles aimed. Water and mud splattered with each galloping hoof. His slicker shined with sliding rain but the Stetson mostly kept his face from getting too damp. His breath came quick with the exertion of keeping the running horse beneath him. Rain roared, a wall of cascading water sucking air with it – the only other sound was the deep drum of the buckskin's hoofs pounding the ground. He saw nothing ahead but more, flat prairie behind a gray curtain of rain.

There was no place to take a stand.

Indians loomed closer, firing twice more, still two hundred or so yards behind. Link reined in the buckskin turning to the right. He swung his right leg over the back of the saddle but kept his left boot in the stirrup while he pulled the buckskin's head around. He pulled hard on the saddle horn.

'Down,' he said. He knelt with both knees aimed toward

11

the wet grass and pulled. 'Down.'

The buckskin fought the pull, trying to stay on its feet. When Link jerked the horn, the horse kneeled then rolled to his left side as Link pulled his foot from the stirrup and flattened behind the saddle.

The Indians wore Cherokee feathers, and rode hard within a hundred yards. Two more shots rang out. A bullet sliced the side of the saddle and seared Link's vest. The buckskin jerked, fighting to stand. Link put his arms on the side of the saddle holding it down. He stroked the horse's neck.

'Settle down now.'

The Cherokee were eighty yards and closing, rifles to their shoulders.

Link rested the Henry on the side of the saddle. He started farthest right and fired. The rider rolled from the saddle, landing on his head and neck. With another load, Link shot the next, then a third. Seeing three Cherokee drop from their horses, the other three peeled off to their right fifty yards out, then turned back and galloped away. Link stood and lined another bare-back Cherokee in his sights.

The buckskin pushed to his feet and shook rainwater and mud off himself. Link waited, peering down the barrel but didn't fire. He stood looking over the saddle through a gray blanket of hard rain, water dripping from the brim of his Stetson. The retreating Cherokee were almost out of sight, riderless ponies running with them. Link slid the Henry back in the scabbard. He walked around the buckskin, wiping his hand over its neck and face.

'You OK?' he asked.

The horse shook his head again. He snorted and pushed his nose against Link's chest.

Link swung up into the saddle. 'They must not know I was married to a Pawnee. I'm practically kin – sort of.'

TWO

Link rode down through flat prairies toward the Santa Fe Trail, headed for Tucson where he thought he might settle while he waited and looked for Spike Carp. He stopped at Fort Sumner to spend the night and made howdy with old time scouts he knew, then moved on.

Ten miles outside the fort was a Hell on Wheels whistle stop called Knot Head Junction, population 1,250. It had three saloons, one hotel, two tent whorehouses, a hardware store, café, livery stable, funeral parlor, a clapboard church with a bible-slapping hell and brimstone preacher, and little-enforced law carried out by an elderly, drunk, town marshal.

Link learned that Spike Carp wasn't in town but that his brother, Pinetop was because he'd heard Link was headed south.

The air in Knot Head Junction was brisk when Link came out of the Drover Saloon on Forelock Road, the biggest and most popular drinking and fighting saloon in town. A gunfight was about to take place on the dusty road, between Fletcher Calvery, from Charleston, wearing a cross-draw .44 Remington rig, and a former slave turned cowhand, Idris Harris, with a high leg hip draw Colt. They faced each other in the middle of Forelock.

Fletcher Calvery said, 'I told you to be gone by morning. We don't want your kind in our town.'

Idris Harris stood with legs slightly apart. 'I figure that was whiskey talking, Reb. You've had a change of mind, thought better of it now. You can still walk away.'

'I ain't thought nothing better of it. No hombre worse than a educated black, 'less it's a whore gets religion. You get outta our town.'

'Not your call, Reb,' Idris said.

'I'll drop you in the dirt where you stand.' Calvery's voice wavered.

Link considered it the voice of a dead man.

'Stop talking and do something,' Idris said.

By the time Fletcher Calvery cleared his holster, Idris Harris had already slapped a slug through the man's heart. He fired again to tear open a lung.

With Calvery face down in the dirt, Idris held his Colt pointed to the ground and looked up and down the crowded road. 'Anybody else?'

Unimpressed men eased back into the three saloons lining both sides of the road, the entertainment done. Link stayed on the wood-planked walk. He waited for the former slave to approach him.

They stood on the boardwalk facing each other. Idris Harris was as tall as Link, maybe thirty-five, skinny with black hair, two scars along his left cheek and three days of beard stubble. He had been watching Link's right hand as he approached. He holstered his own revolver and stood two feet away, black eyes locked on Link's face. 'Fellas around town say you're Link Bonner.'

Link nodded. 'You were a slave once.'

'I was, 'til twelve years ago – 1865, I got a pistol in my hand and put an end to my master. No more masters for me.'

'From Georgia?'

14

'You was a Johnny Reb in that last war,' Idris said. 'You fight for Georgia?'

'I fought for Texas. We didn't care much over problems of the South. We wanted to be a republic again. The war's been over a long time.'

'Some still fighting it.' Idris looked up and down the street. Across the dusty road, two men entered a saloon.. 'You put out the word, Link. You're looking for the Carp brothers. A no-good bunch if ever there was. Bad *hombres*.'

'They raped and mutilated my wife – made me watch before they shot me to pieces.'

Idris nodded. 'They know you're dogging them and in the area. Pinetop Carp is just outside town. He's the second oldest, right? You know the Carps offered a thousand dollars gold coin for your dead body.'

'Offered it to anybody?'

'Whoever wants to take the shot.'

Link said, 'I doubt they got a thousand dollars.'

'That's what I was thinking. But they sent somebody to find you, someone set on starting a reputation. He's here looking for you.'

'I ain't no gunfighter.'

'Maybe you need some help.'

Link said, 'I hear he's young – a cousin or something. The Shorthorn Kid,'

'How do you know it isn't some educated ex-slave from Georgia?'

'I don't. That's why the thong is off my Colt hammer.'

'You think you're fast enough?'

'No, but are we gonna find out?'

'Not if you buy me a whiskey.'

Link held his arm out to the saloon door. 'After you.'

The next evening was a noisy, Saturday night and at the

stable, Link had brushed the buckskin and fed him a handful of oats. He gently patted the side of his neck.

Before he stepped out of the stables for a few hands of five-card stud at the Drover Saloon, he felt the pain of loss pull across his chest. Memories again – even after two years, life without Yana sometimes came hard. They had shared so much while he worked as an army scout out of Fort Union. Her father had been one of seventy Pawnee scouts hired by the army who were never paid their promised money. More government forked tongue. Link scouted for the army month-to-month. When they paid him at the end of the month, they had him for another month. That had been his contract with them.

Link heard movement outside the stable, the squeak of leather against the water trough. He felt a tingle on the back of his neck and shivered. A dim lantern showed little light. His hand shook slightly but he managed to draw the Peacemaker with it.

'Bonner, all your life troubles are over.'

'Good,' Link said as he knelt behind a stack of hay bales. 'They were becoming a burden.'

'You know who I am? The Carp brothers got a message for you.'

Link reckoned his chances of survival grew less the longer the conversation continued. The stable walls were old, pine planks, weather-bleached and thin. 'I got no grouch with you, kid.'

'It's about the money, Bonner. You know it's always about the money. Come out and draw.'

The stable air cracked as Link made the shot through the wall toward the sound of the voice. He jumped ahead from the bales and ran to the door. The Shorthorn Kid stood behind the trough, draped in black and silver, with pearl snap-buttons on his black shirt. He carried Colt .44s on each hip – one sliding out of the holster going for the draw. His black Planters hat tilted back, so his young face shone in the moonlight. Three steps to the door, Link dropped and rolled outside. He shot the Kid through the chest just as the .44 cleared the holster, then two quick shots through the hip and the Stetson. The Kid twisted, dropped the .44 and slumped into the trough. Link lay on his belly, heart pounding, smelling gun-smoke, hearing the snort and cry and stomp of horses and the gurgle of a dying youngster, while a stream of water drained from the bullet-hole through the trough, soon the loudest sound at the stable.

The Shorthorn Kid never got off a shot.

Link Bonner and Idris Harris stood at the bar inside the Drover Saloon, boot heels hooked on the brass rail, glasses of whiskey and the bottle at hand between them. The rumble of men's voices surrounded them. No music or other noise added to the voices – the saloon carried nothing as sophisticated as a piano or banjo.

Three dusty, rough-looking men came in through the batwing doors. Weaving between the crowd of drinkers, with trail-weary eyes on Link and Idris, they went to the end of the bar and ordered whiskey. Link studied them for a sign of recognition – to see if any were Pinetop Carp.

One of them said, 'Since when do they let blacks drink in a saloon with men?'

Idris eased the rawhide loop off the hammer of his Colt.

Link said, 'The war ended years ago, boys. You looking for trouble, it's standing here waiting.'

The bartender went to the end of the bar with the whiskey bottle, leaned across and whispered to the strangers. They looked at each other then looked at Link and Idris. They nodded and slugged down their drinks and stared at the empty glasses.

'Not looking for no trouble,' the trail rider said. 'Just want to wash dust off our throats.' They poured again.

'Then welcome,' Link said.

Idris gulped down his whiskey. 'You put fear in the heart of the brothers, old hoss. They'll have to offer more money now for your demise. They might even get to my price.' He gave Link a wide grin.

'That they probably don't have,' Link said.

'There is that, yes.'

Link slugged down his whiskey. 'I'll be headed out of town. I hear it's a cabin beside some creek or river, about three miles out.'

'Maybe he figures the Shorthorn Kid put you down. Pinetop is supposed to be the fastest draw of the brothers.'

'It won't do him no good,' Link said.

THREE

Pinetop Carp did not live in the cabin alone. Just before sunrise the next morning, Link reined the buckskin into a stand of willows by the river. Fifty yards away, the cabin was a two-room lean-to shack cobbled together by men in a hurry for shelter. Five horses crowded the small corral, just big enough for six.

During the morning, Link watched from the trees as they went in and out of the cabin – to the well and the outhouse; he reckoned three men and a woman. He recognized Pinetop by the bright-red hair sticking up from his scalp and his bulldog face, remembering him from two years ago and the sharp knife in his hand while he went to work on Yana's breast.

Pinetop emerged from the outhouse, pulling up a red suspender over his dirty, gray long-John shoulder when the woman walked toward him to relieve herself. She looked more girl than woman, her face still chubby. She wore a tan calico dress from shoulders to knees and nothing else, her stringy, brown hair hung to her tiny butt. As she passed Pinetop, he patted the little butt and grinned at her.

'None of that,' she said. 'You got to share.'

Link watched the girl go into the outhouse and Pinetop back into the cabin. The rising sun blinked through the willows. He rubbed his mouth, undecided. He squatted by the buckskin and stared at coils of smoke rising from the fire-place chimney. The girl returned to the cabin. Besides burning wood, he smelled fresh coffee and wanted some. He had to decide how he would leave the cabin – all of them dead, or just Pinetop? Link did not intend to draw down on the man. He'd likely surprise or back shoot him – not to kill, but to settle him before the killing got started. The man had to be torn to pieces because of what he'd done to Yana. The others in the cabin? Luck of the draw or circumstance. No way to predict events.

Link heard a man's loud voice – not Pinetop's. 'Nobody gives a damn about privacy, Pinetop. She's just some dumb whore from town. I want my breakfast. You ain't gettin' your poke 'til we get breakfast. Now, dammit, that's how it will go.'

'Let's have breakfast then,' Pinetop said. 'Roxanne, you get some flapjacks going. After, we'll throw these hombres out and have our lovin'.'

Link listened to rattling breakfast hardware. Besides coffee, he caught the scent of maple syrup and wanted some flapjacks too – with butter and syrup. Emma Fitzgerald made a fine plate of flapjacks – and good sausage and scrambled eggs. She was a loving, good-bodied woman with long, cin-namon hair, and enough time to get over the demise of her cavalry-officer husband, so ghosts didn't plague her like they did some widows – not like they haunted the ex-army scout she invited to her fort quarters and her bed. He wondered if she really would follow him as she said. No, the woman had more sense than that.

Such thoughts worked at Link during the cabin breakfast. His stomach growled and his tongue ached for the taste of coffee. No talk came from the table but at least one was a sloppy, noisy eater. He doubted it was the girl.

The meal didn't take long, about five minutes.

20

'Go on, now,' Pinetop said. 'You fellas wait outside. You might feed the horses.'

'This won't take long,' Roxanne said. 'A lot quicker than breakfast.'

The two men ambled outside, both shirtless, suspenders holding up their wool pants, wearing Montana Peak Stetsons. They had hog legs in holsters tied down to their thighs. They shuffled to the corral. In their thirties, one was a skinny pole with unruly black hair. The other had thin, last remnants of yellow hair and a creased, scowling face.

Black hair said, 'I'm next. Ain't no way to talk around it, Cliff. I got Roxanne right after Pinetop.'

'Yeah, Blackie, 'cept we better start thinking on more than a poke with that skinny youngster.'

They began to break up one of the hay bales under the corral shed and spread it around the yard. The horses ate eagerly.

'You mean gunnin' down Bonner,' Cliff said. 'We're gonna have to hit him by surprise. The Shorthorn Kid was fast, real fast. I seen him take two cowhands just outside Waco – maybe a year ago – dropped the pair of them 'fore they fired a shot.'

Blackie stopped and stood up straight, looking at the flowing river. 'What you think Pinetop did to that Bonner fella, get him so riled? He ain't just killing the brothers, he's mutilating them.'

Cliff shook his head. 'I dunno. Bet it's got something to do with Pinetop's tobacco pouch. You ever look at it? I expect maybe we takin' on more load than our ponies can carry.'

'Two-hundred in gold apiece is a load I can manage.'

'We ain't seen it, yet,' Blackie said.

'We ain't done the job, yet.'

'We gonna have to dry-gulch the man. Shoot him down dead before he can blink.'

'We got to do what we got to do,' Cliff said. He looked toward the cabin. 'I think I'll take a shot at her after you're done.'

Grunts and girlish whimpers came from the cabin, growing louder and faster.

Link knew there would be no time for conversation. He checked the buckskin's tether to make sure it was tight enough not to pull loose of the willow due to all the noise that was about to happen. The Peacemaker in hand, he stepped from the trees, and without a word, shot Blackie through the side of his head. The crack echoed off hillsides and moved up along the river through canyons. Cliff clawed for his weapon. Moving toward the corral, Link quickly shot again, hitting Cliff through the side. That paused him long enough for the next bullet to plow through his heart.

The noise of stumbling movements came from the cabin.

'Hey, not so rough,' Roxanne cried.

A minute of silence passed next.

Link moved into the corral among the horses. They snorted and stomped in fear and tried to avoid the bodies but on occasion stood on them. They rolled their eyes, nervous, uncertain.

From the cabin, Pinetop Carp said, 'That you, Bonner?'

Link gripped the mane of a black stallion with his left hand, staying behind the horse, the Peacemaker in his right aimed at the cabin. A mare standing next to the stallion plopped chips close to his boots. Link squinted; his teeth clamped tight, his body stiffened though he knew he had to stay loose. The fresh chips presented an aroma well known. His eyes stared at the front door of the cabin. He was aware something might come around from the back. The hammer of the Peacemaker cocked. He said nothing.

'I'm coming out, Bonner. You better not be quick to

22

shoot.'

The stallion shifted, uncomfortable. It was the most aggressive acting horse in the corral. It stomped, tried to nuzzle the mare. Maybe he read something in the horse chips. Link jerked on the mane, pulling the head back.

'Don't do this,' Roxanne cried.

The cabin door opened. Pinetop's Remington .36 came through first. He followed behind a naked Roxanne, the girl held tight against him. They both looked through the trees and along them and finally saw Link in the corral. Pinetop turned to face the corral, and pulled Roxanne with him. Her girl-face twisted, the big blue eyes shining with fear.

'Please,' she said. 'I got nothing to do with this.'

Link remained silent. She wasn't big enough to protect the outlaw completely. Link fired, his aim just above her right shoulder. The bullet hit Pinetop through the collar-bone, but took a dime-sized chip from the top of her shoulder. She screamed and wiggled from his grasp. Pinetop jerked back and bounced against the cabin door. Roxanne bent and took off at a run for the willows, holding her bleeding shoulder.

Pinetop's Remington hung loose in his hand. Link shot the left collar-bone. The horses jumped and bumped into each other with the noise, no space to step around inside. Sharp hoofs stomped the bodies some more. Pinetop slid down against the door jamb to sit, his weapon in the dirt. Link released his grip on the mane and stepped around the horses and out of the corral. He looked off to the trees. He heard branches break, the noise getting softer as the girl ran away.

Pinetop bled along both arms. He had pants on, but nothing else. He carried a saber cut from the war, across his chest. Link remembered it from watching the man rape Yana.

Link said, 'You still got the tobacco pouch?'

His bulldog face, wrinkled and flushed with pain, jowls floppy, brow furrowed, dark protruding eyes showing constant anger and hate – no eyes to be trusted, ever. 'Do what you're gonna do,' he said.

'No regret? No asking for forgiveness? Your other brothers begged for forgiveness. They cried to me how sorry they were.'

'My brother Spike will see you dead and rotting, just like your squaw.'

Link felt the hate and rage well up inside him from his guts. He clenched his left fist. He wanted to empty the Peacemaker ammunition into that bulldog face. He took a deep breath. 'She wasn't quite dead when you started to carve her breast, was she?'

'I don't even remember.'

'You're gonna remember,' Link said. 'You'll remember until your dying second.'

Link chose the black stallion. He saddled the horse with the cinch as tight as he could make it. While he prepared, he kept glancing along the river in case Roxanne came back for her dress, or something else she'd forgotten. When he was finished with what had to be done, nothing she did would matter.

Gripping Pinetop's ankles, Link dragged him to one of the willows, Pinetop trying to kick loose from the powerful hands. He chose a willow on the edge with plenty of space beyond it. He tied Pinetop's left ankle tight to the trunk. The ugly face watched him with contempt, the man apparently ready to accept whatever happened. Both his arms shined red with blood flowing from his shoulders. His hands did not move. His attitude changed when Link brought out the black stallion. Link tied another knot tight to Pinetop's right ankle.

'Hey, what're you doing?'

Link did not speak. The other end of the right ankle rope he looped tight to the stallion's saddle horn. He mounted the stallion over the strung rope.

'You can't do this,' Pinetop cried. 'You can't.'

'Watch me,' Link said. He heeled the stallion hard with his boots. The horse bucked, then jumped forward one step until forced to stop. Link heeled it again. The stallion lunged forward.

Pinetop screamed in pain. 'Stop!' he cried. 'In God's name, please!'

Link heeled again. This time the stallion went another step forward.

'Please!' Pinetop screamed. 'Stop! I'm sorry! Forgive me! We never shoulda done it! Sorry! Sorry! Sorry!' His scream cut off, gagging on blood.

The stallion lunged forward – pulled and jerked against the rope – three steps, then five, then ten.

Link stopped kicking the sides of the horse. He dismounted and pulled the saddle and dropped it where he stood. He pulled the reins and slapped the stallion's rump. He felt fluttering in his chest but no emotion – as if he was digging a hole in soft earth. At the corral he opened the gate. The other horses exited, following in the direction of the departing stallion. Gripping ankles, he dragged the two shot and stomped bodies into the lean-to cabin. He stood at the table. Taking his time, he picked up and ate two untouched flapjacks, washed down with three swallows of coffee. Using the table lantern, he fired the cabin to burn everything inside, but did not stay to wait for ashes. He did not once glance at the bleeding, split body tied to the willow trunk. He rode away without a backward look at his leavings.

Three left – Bart, Wesley and Spike.

FOUR

Spike Carp felt a shiver run through him when he got word, roundabout from Roxanne of what Bonner had done to Pinetop. It was downright inhuman to kill a man that way. And poor Roby, gutted like that. He shook tobacco from his tanned and processed human-skin pouch onto corn-husk paper for the makings, the pouch smaller than he would have liked. After the roll and tongue swipe to keep it together, he stuck the cigarette between his thin lips and fired it with a wooden match. Just no figuring some men and the way they thought.

Alone, he occupied a table at The Trail to Ruin Saloon along Main just off First, downtown Yuma. He recalled another saloon with a similar name somewhere in Prescott or Globe. Half the tables were occupied by drifters and saddle tramps – they never had enough money for eats, but enough to smoke and drink. He kept his bottle of whiskey with another glass because he was expecting a lady.

Wesley was in Prescott, but would soon be on the way to Williamsport to dry-gulch the used-to-be army scout. Bart stayed in Tombstone playing with his Mexican *señorita*, but he'd be along. Spike was pleased that he and his remaining brothers had resolved their differences – all over nothing – the split from that bank in Bisbee. Since Spike was oldest and had planned the job, it was only natural he should get a bigger slice than the others. They took exception to that. The argument lead to a brawling fist fight and each rode on a different trail.

Too bad for Roby and Cookie and Pinetop. The scout had caught up to them. Things would be different now, the brothers working together once again. Maybe they should be together to meet Bonner. Jump him all at once. He'd think about that. Spike slugged down a swallow of whiskey. Squinting with irritation, he took a final drag on the cigarette, dropped it to the floor and stomped his heel on it. The damn woman was late.

Lillian Bly wore black, buttoned up the front to her throat. She wore her black hair in a bun and had amber eyes. Her face showed itself to the world as almost attractive. Spike Carp noticed the nose had been broken long before. She had a knife scar just above her left eyebrow. The scar covered a worm section where eyebrow hair might have grown – the eyebrows also black. The little that Spike could make out of her frame, she was small on top, but not too wide across the bottom. She pushed thirty hard – maybe went beyond it. She smoked a foul-smelling cigarillo from a silver case carried in her purse.

She fixed Spike with a hard, dark stare. 'You looked me over close as a horse you're buying. You think I can attract the man?'

'Mebbe, if you play your personality right. He's a hard case – took the death of his squaw real severe – used to be an army scout.'

Lillian blew smoke in the air. 'He's just a stage driver now, ain't he? Got no steady woman?'

'He had hisself a widow up in Fort Union. He left her so mebbe she didn't mean nothing. I talked to her but she was too loyal to the jasper – got nothing out of her. No, I don't think he's got a woman now.'

Lillian took a sip of whiskey and made a sour face. 'I like champagne.'

'Ain't no champagne at this table.'

She nodded. 'A man without a woman offers possibilities. I already sense he's broody and distant.'

'All I know, he's deadly and real sick about what he does with men after he shoots them.'

'I'll get close enough to him for my dagger.'

Spike gulped more whiskey and leaned back. 'Don't be so sure of yourself. You're kinda a backup, in case my brothers can't shoot out his lanterns.'

She sat straight with her shoulders back. 'You don't think I can handle him?'

'That's an unknown, Lilly.'

'Don't call me Lilly. It sounds shopworn. Do you have the five-thousand?'

'We settled on three.'

'I get three as a down payment, the other two when the stage driver is gone.'

Spike felt his face flush with anger. 'The bank in Bisbee didn't pay off a whole lot. And I had expenses.'

Lillian leaned forward on her elbows. 'Don't tell me that. I don't care how or where you get the money. When I step away from this table I better have three-thousand in my purse.'

'Fifteen-hundred.'

'Maybe a federal marshal might like to know about Bisbee, and your plan for the stage driver, and what you boys did to his child bride.'

Spike squinted at her, already thinking what a bad idea this was. 'Don't let your greed make you excess – Lilly.'

She sat as stiff as he. Her lips worked, making her look

unattractive to the point of downright ugly. 'Careful. Your shiny, shaved head is sweating. Maybe you better put your hat on.'

Spike relaxed. He sat back in the chair and filled both glasses from the bottle. No need to get upset over the bitch. He had chosen her because of the newspaper article. She had caused a member of the territory governor's staff to leave his wife for her. The wife then took too much opium and died. The staff member had shoved his Colt Navy .36 in his mouth and blown his brains out. Scandal and shock had followed, and Lillian Bly had to get herself out of Phoenix to someplace she was less known. Apparently, she had a string of such incidents trailing along behind her. There had even been talk that she sort of helped the man along in his suicide.

'Three-thousand it is,' Spike said. The other two-thousand would come along when a blizzard covered Yuma in a five-foot blanket of snow. He handed her an envelope with the money inside.

Lillian smiled, which made her look sweet and vulnerable. 'You'll be hearing from me or about me.' She put the envelope in her purse and dropped the unfinished cigarillo in her full whiskey glass. She stood, bent and kissed Spike, wet and solid on the mouth, and walked out of The Trail to Ruin Saloon.

Spike stepped out of the saloon and stood on the boardwalk as Lillian Bly entered The Arizona Hotel. At the hitching post in front of the hotel, Wesley Carp swung down from his roan and gave Spike a wave. Spike pointed inside the saloon and waited for his brother to cross the road. After a handshake, they went in and sat at the same table. Lillian's perfume lingered longer than the kiss.

The saloon had a badly-played piano. Wesley pulled his

Montana Peak Stetson and looked at the bottle still on the table. He had a mop of mahogany hair and was dressed in a blue, wool suit with satin vest under the coat. He wore a cross-draw Remington .36 – and stared at the whiskey glass with the cigarillo in it.

'Let me get a clean glass,' he said. He went to the bar, pounding trail dust with his Stetson and returned to fill the glass. He took a hard swallow then loudly cleared his throat. Another swallow finished the glass so he poured again. 'Female company?'

'With a reputation. She can cut the legs off any man. What happened with your hot tortilla?'

Wesley grinned, looking almost embarrassed. 'She was hot, no doubt.' He rubbed his chin. 'But she went and got herself in a family way. I couldn't see myself listening to the squalling of a little chili pepper so I had to cut her loose. You know how them women are. Once a kid comes, the man don't matter, he's just an afterthought, a nuisance hanging around. He was needed for the seed but not no more. She got real upset when I was packing my bundle – even tried to push a knife in my back. I had to knock her around a bit 'fore I left.'

'There's plenty more around,' Spike said.

'Sure. Who was at the table?'

'A woman I hired to get rid of Bonner.'

'I thought we were taking care of that.'

'Backups and backups – we got to get the man dead. With Christmas coming, we got you in Yuma, Lillian and her romance in Williamsport, Bart along the trail, and me in Mineral City. By God, one of us better see the son of a bitch as dead as his squaw before Santa visits.'

'We ought to jump the bastard as a gang – all of us.'

'I lose one more brother and the plan will change.'

Wesley pointed to the whiskey glass with the cigarillo in it.

'Is that Lillian?'

Spike nodded. 'She's trying to steal from us. When we can work it in, one of us got to stop her breathing, preferably after she takes care of the squaw man – or one of us does.'

FIVE

Mineral City, Arizona Territory, along the Colorado River, December 1876, Link Bonner drove and hauled for *Sid Brace Stage and Freight.* Handling a four-up, Link carried as many as four passengers on the two-day Mineral City to Yuma run, rolling through Rode's Ranch, Dismal Flats – with an overnight stop in Williamsport – then south past Eureka, Castle Dome, Arizona City and on into Yuma – a run of sixty miles. He tried to carry passengers both ways but the ferry still floated across the Colorado, and Wells, Fargo and Butterfield had runs in California wherever anyone wanted to go. The other side of Yuma, Butterfield carried passengers along the Rio Gila River all the way to Tucson and a little beyond, and trains screeched on from there. Other days, Link hauled freight with two mules to supply stops between. Rolling along those roads made him most aware of weather – summer heat and wind; light spring rain; bitter finger-numbing winter cold – and always the Apache, sitting their ponies, watching. Nights were usually spent camped along the trail when he couldn't find a roof.

Sid Brace, twenty-five, handsome with ordinary, brown hair and a long, straight nose, operated his small stage and freight line from the back of his downtown Yuma home. He lived with his plain, child-faced wife, Nellie Jo, three months with child and devoted to Jesus more than any human. Sid had concerns with Link so old at forty-two compared to his other two nineteen-year-old drivers, Max and Alex. – Max with his bib overalls and buck-tooth grin carried goddess worship for Nellie Jo, though she herself was only eighteen, and only loved her Lord. Alex had a square, boyish face with blue eyes and straight, blond hair poking out of a bowler, and wore a tan, pullover shirt with black, wool vest. He had a habit of scratching his right eyebrow with his thumbnail as if he was always pondering something.

The business consisted of three freight wagons and a used Concord Coach made by Abbot, Downing and Company, that had small rips in the velvet seats. For those needing to make the trip, the price was cheap enough, and Link usually carried Sid riding shotgun when one of the freight wagons sat idle. Sid didn't like the young boys bumping against Apaches out on the dusty, rough road. Link had more road experience, plus he was accurate with rifle and pistol, as he demonstrated when teaching the boys.

Given a choice, Link preferred driving the stage to freight wagons. Yes, the four-up team was harder to control than two mules. He also had to listen to Sid complain about his Christian wife who shoved Jesus at him each time he turned around, and showed less affection as her belly grew. But Link liked listening to passengers about the goings-on around the territories. Folks rocked inside coaches from train station to train station, or to areas trains were yet to connect – or the route they took was not yet part of the Butterfield stage line. Rail tracks would cross the Colorado on a bridge the following year.

The passengers came from Boston or New Orleans and were crossing the Colorado from Yuma to the golden west – or north of Mineral City to catch a train, maybe headed up through Oregon and the Pacific Northwest to Washington

Territory. They crossed the country with news that Link added to what he read in the *Arizona Citizen Yuma Edition*, Link eager to learn the latest escapades of the Carp brothers – mostly where they were riding next.

Link didn't know where the three remaining Carp brothers hid out. From what he heard it was someplace between Tucson and Tombstone. He reckoned they might soon make some outlaw move – rob a bank, steal horses, kill and maim and rape – passengers talked, or a small article might show up in the *Citizen*. Once Link knew exactly where they were, he'd make his move on them and finish his brutal business. He held more interest in his brand of justice than any law.

Sitting the stagecoach seat, guiding the four-up, left plenty of space for moralizing – Nellie Jo had Jesus moving around her every other sentence. Link had never been a gospel type man, but he might see the wrong in what he was doing. Most others did. He had three more to go then he was done with it. There was never a question of not doing it, of stopping. He'd head back north to Fort Union for more Indian scouting when the Carp brothers were gone.

The army had pushed the nations to the breaking point already with their arrogance and lies. Link might twist a sliver of truth out of them for all to see. A few mouthy privates and sergeants already called him a stinking Indian lover. His answer to all was the same – silence.

A week before Christmas, Link was in the Sid Brace Yuma stable where he kept his fresh-bought chestnut mare while he drove stage. The mare was older than he wanted but she carried a gentle nature and knew how to run through desert terrain. His buckskin had caught a colic disease and died in its stable stall. Link dragged the Mexican saddle off its perch and slid it over the blanket on the back of the chestnut.

Sid had a light freight wagon run to Gila City. Nellie Jo Brace came out of the house carrying her constant Bible, her belly big and draped with a light-green apron. Her brown hair hung wet as if she'd just come from a bath.

'Link,' she said, 'will you be spending Christmas with us?'

Link cinched the saddle and turned to face her. 'Don't know, ma'am. Got a place to go first, might carry over, and I may have a stage run.'

Her face shined, pudgy, looking mother maternal and no more than nine-years-old at the same time. She stood short as a youngster in a plain-pink cotton dress, throat to ankles. 'We celebrate the birth of our Lord, our Baby Jesus.'

'Yes, ma'am.' Link reached for the hanging reins.

'You don't believe, do you, Link?'

'Never thought much about it, ma'am. Hard enough work staying alive in this world to think about the next.'

'It is Glorious Heaven, not just another world.'

'Yes'm.'

'Will you pray with me?'

'Not today. I got to be someplace else.'

'Max and Alex pray with me. Sid thinks it's just they like the way I smell, but he's not part of the trinity.'

'Probably not,' Link said.

'I don't mean the Holy Trinity. That gives me my spirit. I mean my trinity here on earth, I mean Jesus, my child and me. We have no room for Sid.'

'He feels that.'

'Praise Jesus.'

'Yes'm.' Link had his bundle tied to the back and was about to step up to the saddle. Word had come to him directly from Williamsport that somebody knew the whereabouts of the Carp brothers.

Nellie Jo moved closer. 'Do you think I smell good, Link?'

The saddle creaked as Link swung up. 'Ain't nothing I ever thought about. I got to be moving along.'

She glared up at him, looking ordinary and pregnant.

'You mean to go off drinking and gambling and fornicating with dance-hall girls?'

'Yes'm,' Link said as he eased the chestnut out of the stable. 'I ain't nothing but a man.'

'You need to find Jesus, Link Bonner. Let our Savior into your heart. You must have your soul saved by our Lord, Jesus Christ.'

'Yes'm, I sure as hell need something,' he said as he moved out the corral gate. 'Thank you kindly for the offer.' He reckoned what he needed was to be away.

'Praise Jesus,' she said.

By then he had heeled the chestnut mare to a fast trot.

SIX

Link had ridden out of Yuma and was close to Castle Dome when he caught a glimpse of Bart Carp ready to dry-gulch him. Carp was partially hidden in a boulder cluster with a trickle waterfall. His shot grazed Link's left forearm and sent him out of the saddle to sprawl on his belly in the desert sand.

The air turned so quiet, Link heard the gurgle of the waterfall. The chestnut had stopped five feet away and waited, reins hanging to the ground. When he heard tack noise as Carp mounted his horse, Link eased the Peacemaker from the holster and slid it under his chest, aimed out to his left. He lay on the weapon quietly without moving. He kept his left arm out so sand and dirt blotted the blood. His brain registered the sting of the wound. The Stetson was pulled low, hiding his eyes.

The horse plodded across the trail, went around Link's boots and stopped at the wounded arm. Saddle leather creaked as Bart Carp swung down, his boots scraping the ground. He came over and pushed a toe against Link's side.

'You ain't dead with an arm shot, Bonner. You hit your head on a rock or somethin'? Or, mebbe you just fainted. Could be you're faking. Let's find out.' Carp stepped on the wounded arm and pushed his weight on it.

Link felt searing pain that made him jerk and he fired the Peacemaker, hitting Carp through the boot at the ankle bone. He rolled over to his back.

Carp screamed and jumped, the old Remington jerking to point at the sky. As he brought it down to aim at Link's head, Link shot the gun-arm through the wrist. The weapon flew away while Carp hopped and turned as he grabbed his wrist.

'Aiee!' he cried. He went to his knees, good left hand in the sand grasping for the Remington.

Link got his knees under him. He stood, took two steps and kicked the Remington away. He swung his Peacemaker to smash against the back of Carp's head. One blow wasn't enough so he back-swung to crack a slice across the cheek. Carp dropped like a rug. He didn't go completely out but was woozy enough for no more than fuzzy thinking. He was dressed trail hard – old ragged Union army uniform pants, a wool shirt, a torn brown Stetson and wore the Army Remington low on his right leg. His beard showed growth of a month or more.

Link holstered his weapon and clutched Carp by the collar.

'On your feet,' he said.

'Huh. I can't. My ankle.'

'You heard me.' Link pulled the man to his good right leg. The left boot shined with blood. He dragged him, hopping to keep his bleeding foot off the ground, back across the trail to the waterfall. A stream trickled between boulders, easing down from jagged hills to spill two feet into a pool slightly bigger around than a horse trough and about as deep – deep enough. Willow and juniper grew thick on both sides of the stream, a good spot for a picnic.

Link retrieved the chestnut and tied her next to Carp's horse while he wrapped his forearm with his bandana. Carp leaned against a boulder and watched. Link pulled the weaved, leather lariat from the chestnut, and the coiled, twisted rope from Carp's mount. He dropped them next to the pool. When he reached Carp, he grabbed a handful of his shirt and yanked him from his feet. Carp fell with his knees in the edge of the pool.

'What you doin'?' he said. He still clutched his wrist. Blood oozed between his fingers.

Link pulled off Carp's boots, ignoring the cries of pain which turned to cussing words describing Link's ancestry. He tied the leather lariat tight around both ankles. The left ankle bone looked shattered as a hammered whiskey glass. Link's muscles felt tight and the stabbing pain of his wounded arm made him wince.

The outlaw needed a bath – black, unruly hair shined with filth. Without his hat, Carp looked small and ugly, with beady, dark eyes close together and a small, worm mouth. Link had seen it before while a bare-bottomed Bart Carp had raped Yana. She had said nothing, made no cry until they subjected her to unspeakable acts. Then she screamed – Link, hog-tied to a juniper, forced to watch. He looked away from what they did to Yana. What he studied were the men, their faces. He never wanted to forget.

With the legs tied to a willow so the bare feet almost touched the pool, Link grabbed the wounded wrist. Carp let out another scream. Link tied the twisted rope tight around the chewed flesh and shattered bone, showing no emotion. Despite the screams of pain and insults from Carp, he walked around the pool to the other side, unrolling the rope as he went. He looped the loose end around a willow and pulled, forcing Carp to stretch partway across the pool. He kept pulling until the rope was stretched tight, the arm extended. Carp spit and splashed to keep his head above the water, his good hand treading water. The man turned to float on his back and tried to sit, but the rope was too tight.

Link said, 'Where are your two brothers?'

'Coming for you.' It was hard to stay afloat treading with one hand. The wounded arm stretched above his head, the rope looped to the willow while Link held it tight. Carp's head dipped below the water but he jerked it up, spitting water and coughing.

'Coming from where?' Link asked.

More profanity about Link's ancestry splashed out.

Link said, 'You didn't get a tobacco pouch, did you?'

Carp coughed more. 'Spike did. He likes it a lot, uses it every day – ain't as much fun as how we got it. No wonder you wanted that little squaw with you. Ain't never had nothing so—' He gurgled as his head dipped under again.

Rage boiled inside Link but he suppressed it, pushed it down inside his gut. His grip tightened on the rope. It slipped some but his deerskin gloves kept his palms from burning. He drew the loose end with him back into the pool. He yanked the good right arm above Carp's head as far as it would go – not so that the man lay in the water on his back, but turned over so his face went in. Link tied the rope tight to the wrist then walked back along the ground to another willow trunk, and tied it stretched taut. He sat on the edge of the pool, knees drawn up, squinting as he watched.

Carp had enough strength to arch his back and hold his head above the water for a minute or longer. He no longer spoke. He shook his head and coughed and spit water. The bottom of the pool was just deep enough that his body couldn't touch it without his head going under. He jerked. He tried to swim by kicking his legs but they remained tight. His arms were spread apart enough that he could not turn over – not even to his side.

He sputtered profanity at Link with words not understood. His head went under but he still managed to raise it out – not for a minute, for a few seconds, then his face went down

40

again. He began to pant hard when he came up, spitting more water. Strength left his back first. He could only use his neck to get his nose up enough for a breath. But his jerking and splashing stirred the water. It no longer looked like a placid pool where the trickle-waterfall dropped. Each in and out plop of his head churned wavelets that splashed into his face to fill his nostrils. His head stayed below longer. Neck strength left him. His head drooped under. His body ceased jerking and twisting. He lay half-sunk in the water without moving. The pool became placid around him.

Link mounted the chestnut and rode on out without looking back. He would have to buy another lariat.

SEVEN

Spike Carp figured that if he and his brothers kept on in their pursuit of Link Bonner, they'd end up with no family left. Actually, he was after them, not the other way around. Spike had ridden up from Yuma, on past Mineral City north to Olive City, yet another gold town. When he wired Wesley, he said to meet in a tent saloon, nothing as fancy as board and nails – less conspicuous. He thought about wiring Lillian Bly, but decided to let her get on with her business of contacting Bonner; maybe she might get lucky.

After the two-day ride, Spike entered Olive City – one main road, probably called Main, clapboard assay office, fancy Olive City Hotel, the Downtown Saloon, hardware store, stable – then the tents began. The gold town was laid out much like most, designed to crumble and blow away as part of the desert when the gold ran out. Four tents that were erected out from the structures, wiggled canvas walls.

Spike spotted Wesley's old roan with four other horses tied to the rail in front of a thirty-foot square tent with a scrawled plank sign that called it, the Wet Whistle and Poke Saloon – must have been smaller tents out back for the pokes. Spike reined up and swung down. He tied his mount then used his Stetson to pound trail dirt off his clothes.

Stomping in through the open flap, he spotted Wesley

sitting on half-a-barrel with planks nailed together on more barrels, for a table. The tent had ten of them. A bottle of whiskey and two glasses waited. With such a crowd inside, Spike wondered who was pulling any gold from the hills. He joined Wesley – Wes, his younger brother by one year.

Wes greeted him with, 'The buzzard is popping us off like beer bottles on a fence post.' He filled a glass for Spike.

Wes wore a yellow shirt and black vest, his sleeves pulled up his forearms by black garters.. His Remington holster was tied to his left leg. Since his oval face looked unremarkable, he sported a thick, brown mustache that twisted to a point at the ends – points he kept greased, and that matched the color of his unruly hair. He stared in silence while Spike sprinkled tobacco on paper from his special pouch. He took the offered paper and let his brother add a line of tobacco.

When they had lit and were smoking, Spike said, 'A cavalry detachment out chasing Apache told me they found Bart – not as gruesome as Roby, but the end result was the same.'

'What we gonna do about him, Spike?'

'We ain't gonna do nothing. We gonna make ourselves hard to find. Thing is, Wes, now we got to stick together. We got to have two guns on him if he finds us.' He sipped his drink and watched a plump girl get pawed and manhandled, two half-barrels away. 'Mexico got a few fat banks and wagons to raid. It's pesos but they spend the same. Got *señoritas* feel just as good as that winsome squaw we took. What do you think, Wes?'

'How long we gotta stay?'

'A few months. Give that gal I told you about enough time to work on him – get him romanced right into her dagger.'

'What's her name again?'

'Lillian Bly. She waitin' in Williamsport.'

Both men slugged down their drinks and refilled. They blew smoke at the tent ceiling, already brown from years of burned tobacco smoke.

'That's interesting,' Wes said.

'How so?'

' 'Cause I seen the other one, the skinny one was in Fort Union.'

Spike felt a spurt of surprise slap his chest. 'You mean the widow woman, Emma Fitzgerald?'

'I seen her in Fort Union, but never met her like you. If you talking the widow Bonner shared quarters with, that's the one. She's quartered across the river in Fort Yuma.' He rubbed his hand across his chin. 'I think she's moving down-town.'

Spike sat stiff, felt himself blinking with disbelief. 'Get outta here, no, you don't say. You figure she followed him down here?'

'How should I know?'

'Hell, Wes, this may change things.'

'How so?'

'Suppose somebody was to sweep the lady off her feet and store her someplace? Suppose them same somebodies was to use the little darlin' to flush out a jasper been killin' off a family of good people – even have a little fun with her?'

Wes twisted the end of his mustache, a frown showing under his Stetson. 'She's in an army fort, Spike. She's the widow of a major. You want the cavalry running sabers through us? Besides, there ain't six of us no more, just you and me. And we ain't got the money or personality to recruit a gang.'

'But you know she's gonna contact that Bonner jasper. They was hot and wet up there in Fort Union. I reckon she's maybe down here just for him.'

'We ain't got enough bad hombres to pull it off.'

'We can get money in Mexico, Wes. Then we can hire us some kidnappers.'

44

Wes dropped his spent smoke to the floor and twisted his boot heel against it. 'I think you got derailed, old brother. Snatching and sporting women ain't our priority. We got a killer coming after us. He already ended four of our brothers, and he ain't ready to settle back and run his hand along some nice-shaped leg. He left the woman in Fort Union; he'd just as likely not fool with her in Fort Yuma. The man is on a mission – us. We're his reason for living on accounta what we done to his squaw. You and me got to concentrate on that. He's out to kill us. I even wonder if the two of us together can take him.'

'He ain't no gunfighter.'

'Maybe not, but he sure as hell is a man-killer. And he's killing us in a bad way, a nasty, horrible way.'

'You act like you're plumb scared of him.'

'That's 'cause I got sense, brother. Sense enough to like the idea of Mexico. But there ain't nothin' to say he won't come down there after us. What's to stop him?'

'A romance,' Spike said. He didn't like this kind of talk from his brother. It wasn't sense to be scared, it was weakness. 'We relieve a coupla Mexican banks of their pesos, we can maybe hire us a gang of kidnappers. We can come up here and snatch the good-looking widow.'

'For what return? Bonner ain't got no money. You think the army is gonna pay some ransom for the widow? They likely just ride over us like desert mesquite without a look back or a howdy-do. There's more of them and that makes 'em more dangerous than Bonner.'

'Link Bonner,' Spike said in disgust. 'I'm sick of that name. There wasn't hardly anything in that wagon. We got maybe two-hundred in cash.'

'Plus fringes. You the one said we do it. We was trail-bored and you wanted the diversion. It wasn't about money, it was about fun. Now we paying for that fun. Our brothers already paid.' Wes slugged down a drink to empty his glass. He poured another. He sighed and looked around the saloon, his oval face twisted in frustration, his pointed mustache twitching. 'You're my older brother and I respect you, but most of your ideas ain't no good because we ain't got a big ranch and we ain't wealthy. We get spurts of big money, then spurts of dirt-poor poverty – and we spend most of our time running from something. If it ain't the law, it's a gut-mad, ex-army scout on account of what we done to his young bride.'

'Is that why you split from me?'

'That's part of it – hell, most of it. Mostly it was you got too greedy on the Bisbee job and took too much. But our breakup let the scout pick us off one at a time. I don't like no kidnap of no army widow just for sport and maybe not enough return to wet our whistle.'

Spike mashed his spent smoke with his boot. 'Okay, Wes, what you think we ought to do?'

Wes sighed deeply. He flicked the end of his mustache. 'I like Mexico for a few months – give the dagger lady enough time to maybe start a romance. Something else we might consider. If we get us a bank in Mexico, we might hire a local assassin, somebody come up here and pick him off. The man drives a stagecoach. He's pretty much got the same trail over and over. Sure, he's lookin' for us but in the meantime, he's got to eat. If this Lillian Bly can get him to look on her with hot eyes and a rise in his britches, that solves our problem. Otherwise we come back in the summer or fall, rested with maybe some pesos in our pockets, enough for a coupla mean *vaqueros* and together we can dry-gulch him. Hell, he might even start up with Emma Fitzgerald again. Get his heart so fluttered; he'd be weak and easy to take.'

'I'll buy tickets to see that,' Spike said. 'But it could work to a triangle. The two women both wanting what the scout can give them.' He poured whiskey in his glass to empty the bottle, ignoring the buzz he felt. He shook his head. 'That Lillian Bly is rough as a desert pinnacle. She got some miles on her, hard miles. Now, Emma has a way about her, soft, gentle – and she talks like she wants to hook up with the scout permanent. She's got the shape and good looks and sweet manner, better than the dagger lady.'

EIGHT

Monday morning in Yuma, Link had a full coach ready to roll out toward Mineral City with an overnight in Williamsport. Alex and Max loaded the last of the luggage. Alex would ride shotgun, while Max ogled cow-eyed over the pregnant wife. Sid Brace had taken a freight load to Gila City. Passengers in the coach were a drummer who sold crushed buffalo skulls as fertilizer to dirt farmers, and a railroad engineer, entertained by two precious school teachers headed back to work after being home for Christmas – one taught in a small school in LaPaz, the other got off at Mineral City. Their sparkle lit up the inside of the coach, young and bubbly with peachy skin, wide innocent eyes and constant chatter. They kept the men around them smiling, especially Alex.

As Link separated the reins for the four-up, he saw two cavalry soldiers and a woman in a buckboard pass and pull up in front of the Arizona Hotel. He stared at the woman, feeling a slight flutter of memory, and maybe a hint of excitement. One of the soldiers held her hand as she stepped from the wagon to the boardwalk. The other soldier pulled luggage.

Emma Fitzgerald, widow and former resident of Fort Union, New Mexico Territory.

He turned to Alex. 'Hang on here a couple of minutes,' he said.

Alex scratched his right eyebrow with his thumb-nail and followed Link's gaze across the street to the hotel. 'We're runnin' a little behind as it is.'

'This won't take long.'

Across the street, Link nodded to the soldiers returning to the buckboard. He went into the hotel. Except for Emma and the clerk, the lobby was empty.

'Hello, Emma,' he said.

She faced him and stood straight and blinked her dark, indigo-blue eyes – dark to being almost black – wide in surprise. Then she looked pleased. She wore a gray travel-dress with hoop, white lace at the cuffs, and buttoned to her throat. She had a sharp-boned face and a figure to draw attention wherever she went. Her cinnamon hair flowed straight down her back. She took a step as if to hug him, then paused, her look uncertain. That changed while she looked at him boldly.

'Link, I want to be in your arms.'

Link took her elbow and guided her across the lobby, out of earshot from the clerk, aware of her pleasant scent. He stood with her next to the fireplace. When she stepped close, he backed off. 'What are you doing here?'

'I said I would follow you.'

He wasn't irritated. She looked good and it pleased him to see her again. He remembered that perfume intimately, like spring rain – but this was foolish. 'You shouldn't have, Em.'

Her full lips tightened and she stood with her hands on her hips. 'Lincoln Bonner, I'll follow you to heaven or hell. Understand this – the first time I saw you – a scout at the officer's dance – when you entered, you sucked the air right out the room. You sure left me breathless. If I had met you before the major, there never would have been a wedding. If

I'd met you while married to the major, I would have left him. I don't know why – I can't figure it, or care about the why of it. It just is. That's how I feel about you. I came to Yuma because it's where you are.'

'Don't do this, Em. I left you in Fort Union, I'll leave you here.'

'Tell me you haven't once thought of me since you came here.'

Link sighed. 'I can't say that.' He took her right wrist and placed her palm on his chest. 'Feel that. It's hollow because there ain't nothing there – no feelings, no hope, no future – certainly no love. I ain't got nothing to give you. You can't draw from me what don't exist.'

Emma yanked her hand away and threw her arms around his neck, pushing tight against him. 'Put your arms around me.' When he hesitated, she grabbed his forearms and wrapped them around her waist while she pushed harder. Her arms went back around his neck, her lips close to his ear. 'You need a woman, Link. You need her softness. You need her with you for soft conversation in front of the fireplace, mutual secrets, rides out for picnics, shared entertainment and experiences – a woman to hope with and plan with – a woman who believes in you and what you do. Feel me against you. I feel good, I know. You need what a woman can do for you – what I can do for you, especially at night. I got all the love you can handle. When you reach out I'll be there – every time – any place. I know you're capable. I've seen it in your eyes. Not always, but caring and softness often enough to make me know. You ache over your loss, filled with vengeance against those that done it. If you love anything right now, it's the revenge. You love the *need* for revenge you feel. But that will pass, my love, and I will be there. You know I'm a woman and I can give you everything a woman has. You know that because you remember it from Fort Union.'

Despite himself, Link felt his arms tighten. Her body felt far too good, which got stirrings boiling. Her cheek was against his. She worked her lips around until they melted into his and she tasted peppermint-sweet with a hint of morning coffee, her lips soft as her body tight against him, her tears on his cheek. When he pushed away, he breathed heavy. She was a total woman, nobody needed to tell him that. He said, 'Lord, Em, you got my kettle perkin'.' He glanced at the hotel front door. 'But, I have to go. We got to talk later. Are you here in the hotel?'

'For now. I found a small house northwest about five blocks from town, along the river. How long will you be away?'

'The run takes two days each way.'

'The fifth day – Friday, you will come to dinner. I'll be moved in by then. Look the small house over and look me over and think about moving in. Your place will be there.'

'I'll make it to dinner,' Link said. 'Then we'll see.'

'Yes, we will. I'll make you want to stay.'

Emma went up to her room. As Link walked past the counter to the hotel front door, a man approached from the left. Link's first instinct was to reach for the rawhide loop over the .45 hammer. He looked at the man closer.

'Link Bonner? Name is Cecil Castro, just rode down from Mineral City. Been up all night and I'm as tired as my horse.' He stood about five-six; the Stetson gave him another four inches. His eyes were so bloodshot it was hard to tell the color. He needed a shave and sported a cookie-duster that needed to be trimmed.

'Buy you a coffee?' Link asked.

'No, thank you – my back teeth is floating already. Hear-tell you was driving a four-up stagecoach north along that spine-snapping road.'

Link smiled. 'Ain't even got a name. No sketch or map shows it, but we're a small outfit – Butterfield or Wells, Fargo won't touch it.'

Cecil Castro nodded as he looked up at Link. 'I stayed awake so I could warn you. There's trouble up north.'

'Bandits?'

'Apache. I work a gold claim out of Rode's Ranch. I come in for some vittles and ammunition. Eight of them jumped us at the ranch. I figured Chiricahua. Only two had rifles. We picked off a pair of them but they got themselves two more Winchesters and three steers.'

Link frowned. 'Chiricahua – their reservation is out by Globe.'

'I know. These was young bucks. We reckoned they was getting belly-filled and fortified to join that troublemaker Geronimo in Mexico. That outlaw ain't no hero – every time he jumps the reservation, them soldier-boys ride through with a massacre – mostly women and children. He keeps on like this he'll exterminate his own people, who lately don't think much of his shenanigans.'

Link opened the door. Across the road he saw Alex and the passengers waiting. 'We'll be carrying extra artillery.' He held his hand to Castro. 'Much obliged for the warning, Cecil. You heard anything about the Carp brothers? I got word they might be in Mexico.'

'Spike and Wesley. Hear they crossed the border back north.'

'When?'

'Can't say. They got four Mexican bandits riding with them. They held up a stagecoach rolling out of Tombstone.'

NINE

Along the road to Williamsport, the stagecoach rocking while the four horses loped along, Link had much to ponder. No need to head for Mexico to kill the final two brothers. He was liable to have them and their friends sitting on his lap before long.

He thought about Emma Fitzgerald, and remembered how she treated him at Fort Union – treated him better than he deserved, spoiled him. There sure wasn't anybody else lined up to spoil him. He still carried the memory of Yana – but he had to admit, current events crowded that memory. Those who killed her didn't deserve life. He had to make a decision before he returned to Yuma. He liked the idea of intimacy with loving Emma more than trail riding on a hunt through hostile country – with ambush waiting through every town and village. But they had to stop breathing. The final two had to meet the end of their lives weeping and gargling, as they died a bad and horrible death.

In the past, driving stage along the rough road, Link had seen plenty of Apache. He rolled by their wikiup and tepee-cluttered villages – some villages had permanent wood buildings though the Apache were generally nomadic, unlike the Hopi and Navajo who farmed the land.

Link had also driven around cavalry patrols, the soldiers

clanging around in their horse tack, after stray Mescalero who wandered from reservations. The *Citizen* reported that since the great Apache chief, Cochise, was dead, young braves listened to and followed a warrior called Geronimo, who had recently escaped into Mexico to raid and pillage. Many skirmishes broke out, with the Apache usually outnumbered. They watched the cavalry – and Link driving the stagecoach – with suspicion, their Winchester rifles in hand.

A government campaign was underway to take all weapons from Apache, eager Indian agents willing to enforce and execute any law against the hostiles. A law had passed that dropped Indians as nations – the new law stated they were displaced wards of the government – the government could do anything they wanted with them. The army built forts and had been harassing Mescalero and Chiricahua since the 1840s. Army brass and most men considered them an inferior race, not worthy of respect.

White eyes that Link talked to thought the final solution for the Indian problem was extermination. Link carried pity for all Indians. They were a lost people headed for oblivion, a part of historical evolution. In the distant future, pathetic little groups might fight to maintain their heritage, but their time of power and dignity had passed.

And hostile Apache may be waiting up ahead.

In Williamsport, Link reined the tired four-up in front of the Golden Hotel where passengers checked in. One school teacher went to the one-room school where she had an attached apartment.

Alex with his unruly, straight, blond hair under the bowler, aimed straight for the other teacher – almost three years older – and made his boyish gestures. Her name was Millie, a plump gal with a cherub face quick to laugh. Alex made her agree to dinner at the café around the corner. He told Link he didn't want to be in the hotel restaurant with him and the other passengers – they might judge his moves.

With the horses taken care of, Link had a short nap in his room then cleaned up for dinner. The hour was seven and the hotel restaurant was full with rich gold-mine owners. He was directed to the bar to wait. After rolling all day with wind and sun, the enclosed rooms felt stuffy and too warm with tobacco, perfume, and unwashed body smells. Smoke clung to the ceilings and walls. The carpeted floor was dotted with the stain of tobacco spit. Talk came low, mostly from men.

Link got his table. He had one glass of expensive, Kentucky bourbon, which would be his only one, and ordered the beef stew with buttermilk biscuits and a mug of beer. Before the food came, he polished off the bourbon and swallowed his first sip of beer. A woman swished close by his back then came around and sat across from him.

'Hello, Link. The tables are crowded. May I join you?'

Link frowned. 'Do I know you?'

'I must get to Mineral City. Do you have room in the coach?' She wore purple, a little daring in the bodice, showing the bare top mounds of her breasts. She might have been taken for a soiled dove except the dress looked expensive. Her amber eyes reflected like mirrors. She had a scar that replaced part of her thick, dark, left eyebrow. She looked attractive except for certain wrinkles and the hardness in her eyes.

'Just lost a passenger,' Link said. 'We got an empty seat. You can get a ticket at the desk.'

'The desk clerk told me you were the stagecoach driver. I had to have your permission before he'd sell me a ticket. I really need to be on that stage. I'll do anything.' She reached out and placed her hand on his. 'I mean, anything, Link. I was attracted to you right off. I'd like to really show my gratitude.'

Link squinted at her. 'Keep your gratitude. Not needed.

I'll talk to the desk clerk.'

'I'd still like to show how much I appreciate it. Will you allow me to buy dinner, if I can join you?'

'It's crowded, yes,' he said. 'No need to buy. How do you know me?'

She smiled and that sweetened her face right around. 'I heard you were the driver. And I liked the look of you.'

Link puzzled how he'd received so much feminine attention in one day. 'What are you drinking, young lady? You got a name?'

She kept her hand on his and smiled. 'I'd like a glass of champagne, Link. My name is Lillian Bly. You can call me Lilly.'

Link did not bed Lillian Bly.

It was easy to compare her offer to the invitation from Emma Fitzgerald. One came aggressive and crude. The other brought much more than a quick romp similar to what a man paid for in a room above saloons. Lilly had too many glasses of champagne that he made her pay for. When he told her good-night, she clung to his arm up the stairs to his room. His final good-night came when he told her they rolled out at dawn, then he shut the door in her face. He didn't much care for her attitude or manner.

On the hotel bed he dreamed of how Em felt against him, and her words. That brought memories of their time at Fort Union. When the business with the Carp brothers had finished, he would no longer drive a stagecoach or likely stay in Yuma. He might head on across to Tucson, or up around Santa Fe – go back to scouting for the army. He might even work his way back to head scout, supervising Indian trainees.

Would Em be with him? If not, would she actually follow him where he went? The major had left her a tidy sum plus a small, monthly widow payment came from the army. She carried a skill for sewing quilts and only needed discarded clothing and thread to work her trade. They sold from wherever she lived, and sold well. The fine-looking woman didn't need Link, not to get by in life. But she wanted him. And as much as she could in a hotel lobby, she impressed him by what she offered. He couldn't offer much. Maybe in time when his thoughts weren't crowded by Yana, who spoke little and worshipped him, and the brother business was done, he might be capable of caring.

When the predawn knock came on the door, Link realized he had not once during the night thought of his champagne-drinking, dinner companion, Lillian Bly.

The road to Mineral City took longer because it wandered away from and back to the Colorado River. Strewn with rocks and chuckholes, it beat up coach parts without mercy – a rough way to go. Link took it easy, keeping the team at a trot or walk. But he couldn't smooth the coach ride despite extra spring leaves. The school teacher became sick and he had to stop for rest more often. Alex had had himself a long night with Millie the teacher and dozed as much as he could. So, Link reckoned the night had been worth it because they both paid now – Alex weary, and sharp as a ball riding shotgun, and Millie sick with after-effects of demon drink – and who knew what else?

The lunch break at Dismal Flats with hotel-made ham sandwiches came an hour-and-a-half past the noon hour. At the pace they rolled, the stage wouldn't get into Mineral City until almost midnight. Link couldn't pick up speed because the road began to twist and became rougher up ahead – and impossible to see after dark. He hoped to get past Rode's Ranch before the sun went down.

A band of six Apache started to follow the stagecoach.

They stayed a quarter mile back. No war paint but that

meant nothing with so few numbers. It also might have meant that if a raid came, it carried no spirit approval – it was for pure greed and without honor. Four carried Winchesters – the two youngest had bow and arrows.

Link did not want to brace them on an open road from the cover of a stagecoach. Boulder cropping loomed on the river side, some as big as a railroad car. He searched the boulders for an opening big enough to drive the stagecoach through. When he found one so tight the doors barely opened enough for the passengers to squeeze through so he told them to get out. Alex had his twelve-gauge double-barrel shotgun plus he brought a rifle and one of three Colt Navy pistols. He gave one Colt each to Millie and Lillian. Millie made no conversation but tears of terror flowed down her pudgy cheeks while she sniffled.

Link saw the braves had moved to within a hundred yards. They sat their ponies watching. The engineer, dressed in a blue, wool suit with a small, brimmed hat, watched them with Link. He carried his own Remington .44. He told Link he wished for a rifle. The drummer was the oldest of the group and the fattest. He carried only a Derringer so Link gave him the extra Colt. Link had his Winchester '73 and his Peacemaker. They stood behind two boulders with enough opening to see. Lillian Bly stared at Link without expression.

'I can't shoot them,' Millie cried. 'I just can't.' She held the Colt loose in her hand.

Alex moved behind her, put his hands on her elbows. 'Wait until one is coming for you. Cock the hammer and point at him with both hands holding the weapon. Move your arms straight out, close your eyes and pull the trigger. Cock the hammer. Open your eyes. If you missed, do it again.'

'What do they want?' the drummer asked.

Link moved to the other side of the boulder. He rested the Winchester and aimed at the braves. It was mid-afternoon, sunny and comfortable, a breeze slipping up to wind. Sweat came from anticipation and fear. 'They want four things – us dead, rifles and pistols, what little money is between us, and the women.'

'Oh, God,' Millie said.

Link said, 'If we keep shooting and hitting them, they might get discouraged.'

A rifle shot echoed along the boulders. The drummer's head snapped back with a bullet hole through his forehead.

Millie screamed.

Link and Alex fired at the same time, dropping two of them. The engineer took aim while the braves rode for the cover of a jagged rock outcropping twenty feet high. Another dropped from his horse.

'Ah!' the engineer gasped as he jerked. The bullet had pierced his heart.

A brave came riding toward them, his rifle to his shoulder, working the lever as he fired one shot after another. Bullets chipped pieces of boulder, plunked into the coach. Others fired with a staccato of snaps. Link fired and missed. Alex hit the brave in the leg. Millie stood holding her Colt at arm's length, closed her eyes and fired. The brave rolled back off his pony. She opened her eyes and sniffled and cocked the hammer and raised the Colt again.

Lillian came close to Link, looking out beyond the boulders. She breathed hard, her breath coming in pants. She tried to push close to him but he elbowed her away. He saw one ride out from the jagged rocks, bow string pulled to his shoulder. He raised his rifle. He saw the flash of a dagger. It swung down to his chest. He put up his arm and caught the cutting blade across his left forearm. She grunted with the effort, making animal sounds, stood tall, raised her arm and swung the blade again. He gripped the knife wrist and popped her misshapen nose with the barrel of his revolver.

She jerked back.

'Die Bonner!' she screamed. She wriggled her wrist to get free of his grasp. Her nose bled. 'I have to kill you!' she screamed.

Alex turned toward them and raised his aim at her.

An arrow thumped into her back. The sharp arrow point pierced out from her heart. She slumped against Link. He eased her to the ground.

Alex shot the brave.

The one remaining Apache rode off, fast as his pony could carry him.

Alex leaned with his back against the boulder breathing hard and loud with the excitement. Millie ran to him and wrapped her arms tight around his neck. He patted her back and looked from Link to Lilly's body and back again. He stared at Link's bleeding forearm.

'Holy Christ, Link,' he said. 'What just happened here?'

TEN

The fancy-dressed Mexican bandit, Pasco Rodriguez, his jangling spurs ringing with each step, irritated Spike Carp to the point of gunplay. The other three were easy to keep in line. But Rodriguez didn't like the cut from the stage holdup, or that they were camped in wilderness – Spike reckoned the tortilla didn't even like who was in charge.

Another thing was the black man who sat off by himself.

The camp was on a bluff about a mile out of a village called Mesquite, northeast of the Aqua Dolce. Balls of the mesquite plant grew thick across the windy desert down and away from the bluff. There was no water nearby and their canteens drained fast. And the wind blew.

Spike Carp said, 'Okay, you got something scratching your craw, say how you'd make it better.'

Pasco Rodriguez hooked his thumbs under his elegant gun-belt while his wide-brimmed sombrero rocked in the wind. '*Señor*, you say we take a bank in Yuma. Now you say we don't take a bank in Yuma. You say we kill this man – this Link Bonner.'

'That's why me and my brother Wes there, hired you.'

'I want to take the bank in Yuma.'

Spike sighed then said, 'You no longer matter.' He drew and shot Rodriguez through the sombrero and again through the heart. The gunshots echoed across barren flats and bluffs carried by the stiff wind off into oblivion.

The Mexican jerked back to the edge of the bluff and went sliding over. The other three Mexicans stared at Carp with hands on their revolvers but did not draw. He swept his aim at them. He couldn't remember or pronounce their names. Only one spoke English, the others talked just Mex. The black man sat on a rock with the gun in his hand resting on his left leg. His eyes never left Carp's weapon.

The three Mexicans clambered over the edge of the bluff to collect valuables from the body.

Wesley Carp stood by his brother. 'Maybe that wasn't too smart, Spike. We got one less gun now.' He rocked in the wind, holding his hat on his head. The two brothers turned to stare at the black man.

Spike went over to him. The man had beard stubble, looked about thirty-five, with two scars across his left cheek – and was black as coal. 'Idris Harris. Tell me how good you know this polecat, Link Bonner.'

Idris looked down at his boot tops. 'The Link is short for Lincoln.'

'Get on outta here. No foolin'? You mean after the departed president?'

Idris looked up at Spike's face. 'You just killed a man. That don't mean nothing to you?'

'What man? He was Mexican – they ain't no better than Apache.'

'Or you,' Idris said.

When Spike reached for his weapon, Idris had already aimed at his face. 'Careful you don't go the same way.'

Spike stopped midair. He stood with legs apart. He knew the man shot straight and decided not to push it. Wes moved to his right, his hand on the butt of his own weapon. Nobody stirred.

Spike said, 'I ain't drawing down on you.'

'Wise thinking.'

Wes said, 'Let's get civilized, we all after the same thing.'

Spike stepped around Idris' boots and sat next to him on the rock. 'Where'd you meet Bonner?'

'In a cow-patty lump called Knot Head Junction.'

'You know him well?'

'We each left a body there.'

'Yeah, that's when he went after brother Pinetop – Jesus – split him in two.'

Idris squinted at Spike. 'You still got that special tobacco pouch? Pinetop had one too, didn't he?'

'What you sayin'?'

'What some men deserve.'

'He'll get what happened to his squaw.'

Idris shook his head. 'You won't kill him without me. I'm the only way you get to him.'

'How come? What you got against him?'

'Not a thing. I'll kill him because of what you pay me.'

Spike slapped his knees. 'Payment for killing don't work out too good for me. The last one was supposed to sidle up to him and bring out pepper in his pants and get him panting so's she could stick him with a dagger.'

'What happened?'

'An Apache arrow did her in.'

'What did you pay her?'

'Well, we never quite agreed. It was about three-thousand dollars.'

'I'll cost you about five-thousand.'

'I ain't got that kinda cash.'

Idris nodded to the Mexicans climbing up the bluff. 'You can get it.'

'Mebbe. What will it buy me?'

'I draw down on him, shoot him dead.'

'We was gonna kidnap his woman.'

'What for?'

The Mexicans stood apart and talked low in Mexican. Spike didn't like it. He didn't care for the deal the black man offered either. He said, 'You sound like Wes there. It wouldn't be much ransom – who would pay it?'

'Then I repeat, what for?'

Spike shrugged. 'Maybe for sport – we could all take a turn, might be fun.'

Idris squinted at him. 'Looking for more tobacco pouches?'

Spike Carp laughed so loud he rocked back and forth slapping his knee. 'You know, Blackie, that ain't a bad idea.'

Idris sat stiff. 'A slip of the tongue like that can get you killed.'

Spike sat stiff and still. 'Don't mean nothing by it. You know how things are.'

Idris looked out across the windblown mesa. 'Looks like you got to find a flow of cash.'

'Yeah, don't it, though?' To the Mexicans, he said, 'Won't be a bank in Yuma, *señors*. We gonna hit one in Gila City. Then we got this jasper to gun down.'

'Might be Bonner will kill you all,' Idris Harris said.

ELEVEN

In April, Nellie Jo gave birth to a baby girl she named Trinity. By the first of June she had left Sid and went off to Salt Lake City where she joined up with the Church of Latter Day Saints and turned herself into a Mormon. Link reckoned she finally found the earthly trinity she wanted. The church wiggled paperwork to get her divorced from Sid and she became wife number four to one of the elders, who she didn't have to see too often and that seemed to suit her disposition.

Link didn't miss the pudgy youngster, but Sid Brace became morose.

'What did I do wrong?' he asked Link one summer evening.

'Her plans just didn't include you, Sid.'

'But Trinity is my little girl. I got rights.'

'You want to go up against the Mormons, bring plenty of guns.'

'She can't do this, Link, she just can't.'

'She done it. To some women, just being a man with a man's ways is enough to set 'em off. You best find somebody else more in keeping with the way men are.'

'But I love Nellie Jo.'

'Dead love ain't new, Sid. She don't love you, mebbe never did.'

Sid's new love became the whiskey bottle and they were intimate often.

Link Bonner moved in with Emma Fitzgerald to share her small house. Their life became much as it had been in Fort Union. What changed was Link's attitude. He found himself looking at her with a smile – the curve of her jaw, her eagerness with him at night, quiet conversation while she sewed – about her quilt customers, about his stage passengers. Living with Em made him feel good.

When Link wasn't driving stage, he asked around Yuma, Mineral City and Williamsport saloons for any word on the two remaining Carp brothers. He read the *Citizen* in case they were back to attacking wagons and banks. He read about the holdup in Gila City, with Wesley wounded and two Mexicans killed. The gang was off someplace licking their wounds.

June moved three weeks toward July with a relentless sun cooking the land. Link continued driving freight wagons and the stagecoach. Business slowed with the heat, and with Sid's love affair with the whiskey bottle. The bucktooth lad, Max had to be let go, but young, frisky Alex with his bowler and wild blond hair, was kept on as shotgun rider aboard the stagecoach and to handle one of the freight wagons. As the other two wagons were about to be sold, Sid Brace met a wispy school teacher from Atlanta named Sue-Ellen Gulf, got himself divorced from the whiskey bottle, and hired Max back to help drive wagons.

Sid was in love.

Link met Sue-Ellen during the Fourth of July weekend. No stagecoach or freight wagons rolled on the holiday. Sid Brace used one of the freight wagons to collect the school teacher from the boarding house about a mile out of town. They intended to picnic then watch the parade from the front of the hotel. Link heard the marching band while drinking whiskey inside The Trail to Ruin Saloon, one of several saloons he had visited, wishing he had ridden up to Mineral City to continue his search for the Carp brothers – and wanting Em by his side. Emma had an appointment for a quilt sale and would meet him later.

The bartender looked bent and mousy with watery, gray eyes and thin, wispy hair the color of mud. He didn't have to be tough because he kept a double-barrel, sawed-off, twelve-gauge shotgun under the bar and knew how to use it – as a booming weapon or a club. Customers were already half in the bag but steered clear of the bartender called Mars.

Link slugged down a decent glass of whiskey as Mars walked by, dragging his bar rag along the counter.

'Mars,' Link said. 'You hear anything of the Carp brothers in these parts lately?'

Mars stopped. His watery eyes looked Link over from chest to Stetson. 'What you want with the Carp brothers? They likely holed up healing.'

As Link stepped out of the saloon looking for Emma, he saw young, rowdy, drunk, out of work bachelors had their antlers extended for any young woman not escorted, and had been eyeing each girl with interest and comments. The comments worked around what the fresh flower needed to make her quiver, somebody manly and wild to teach her how to please like a real woman. Apparently, the boys didn't have the price of a poke, and had run out of drinking money.

Link watched three of them stagger outside the batwing doors, bunched together, dressed rough and dirty, peach fuzz faces and soiled hat brims low over their eyes. They stumbled along the wooden walk from the saloon toward the hotel, eyes and mouths busy. The band played as it marched along.

The mayor led the parade.

The just-elected marshal – Rupert Howell – marched on the mayor's left. He looked robust enough not to have seen his shoes in a decade. His thick, gray hair hung out and long without a hat. He smiled and waved to bystanders with the attitude of a politician. Rumors had spread that the election was rigged and he'd appointed two mean-looking gunfighters as deputies. Link didn't know or care about their names. He stayed clear of the bunch. They'd been no help seeking the Carp brothers. Behind the marshal came the fire department chief. Noisy children ran back and forth across the road. Folks stood along the route in sparse gatherings.

The young drunks from the saloon reached the hotel just as Sid and Sue-Ellen stepped out, her hand on his arm. Link watched Emma coming across the road toward him. She had red, white and blue ribbons weaved through her cinnamon hair and looked lovely.

Like cattle, the two, weak-minded lads followed what they considered a strong leader. His name was Eddie Bartlett. He might have been almost twenty. In the saloon, Link had noticed Eddie didn't need many drinks to get a snoot on, and he wore an old, Colt Navy .36 cross-draw. His two younger friends, called Willy and Woody were also armed. Both looked just under twenty. Willy was a red-faced, scrubby blond with shifty, green eyes. Woody came from Mexican heritage and appeared the most submissive of the three. Eddie and the boys approached Sid and Sue-Ellen and surrounded them. Sid moved Sue-Ellen in front to his left side.

Link stepped within four paces while he watched Emma reach the boardwalk. He drew his Peacemaker and held it by his leg, pointed down.

Brave Eddie stared at Emma. 'Well, now what sweet, little morsel we got here? Patriotic ribbons in her hair.'

'Yeah,' Willy said.

The brass band played loudly as it marched by. People on the wood-walk waved American flags. One block away, fire-crackers snapped, sometimes in staccato pops.

'Move it along, boys,' Sid said. His young, handsome face showed no fear, just concern.

Emma stepped up on the boardwalk and stopped in front of Sid and Sue-Ellen.

The drunks turned their attention to Sue-Ellen. Bartlett said, 'What we got under that dress, sweet face.'

Link stepped to them, the Peacemaker hammer cocked. Sue-Ellen edged closer to Sid, hooked her arm in his. She showed a face of Deep-South innocence. Her bright-yellow dress extended from ankles to open just below her throat, and clung tight from her bodice to a corseted, tiny waist. Chestnut hair held by a red, white and blue ribbon, shimmered as it fell to her shoulder blades. Flush, red cheeks, a pert nose, and big, brown eyes that looked terrified.

The two boys were on each side of the couple. Eddie Bartlett stood between Sue-Ellen and Emma, openly looking Sue-Ellen up and down.

Sid followed with his eyes as Link moved behind Bartlett.

Link stepped to the young man's right side. 'Afternoon, Sid,' he said. 'Ma'am.'

Emma turned and hooked her arm in his. She kissed his cheek.

Link smiled at her. 'I like your hair.'

Eddie Bartlett turned to face Link, his young, drunk face wrinkled in anger. He looked down at the Peacemaker pointed at his stomach. 'I'm the meanest hombre along this main road. I can chew up guns and bullets. I ain't nobody to mess with. What you think you gonna do?'

'Stop you from bothering the ladies with your crude behavior.'

'Stop me?' He squinted at the Colt .45 aimed at him. 'It

ain't just me, in case you didn't notice, old man. There's three of us.'

'Once I kill you, these other two will pee their pants.'

Sue-Ellen lifted her brown eyes enough to look at Link. Emma remained still, pushed against his left arm.

Sid grinned and said, 'Sue-Ellen, I'd like you to meet my lead stage driver, Link Bonner, and his lady, Emma Fitzgerald.'

Link touched his hat brim with his left hand. 'Ma'am.' Emma and Sue-Ellen nodded to each other, nothing more.

Bartlett stood stiff, his back straight, drunk, bloodshot eyes confused. He stared at Link.

Sid went on. 'Link, after you drop the loud mouth, you'll have to hit this other one. I'll take care of what's left.'

Link said, 'Why don't you boys just stagger along and stay out of trouble.' He took a step closer to Bartlett. 'Unless you want your liver ripped.'

The band had marched past and was rounding the corner, still playing. More firecrackers popped down the block.

'No,' Bartlett said. 'Maybe we will move along.' He turned away from Link.

Link said, 'After you apologize to the ladies.'

'Huh.'

'I heard remarks you made we all took as insult. You owe the ladies an apology.'

Bartlett turned back to face Link, his lips working to show his rage. 'Don't push it.'

Sid moved Sue-Ellen a little apart. 'Whenever you're ready, Link.' He stared at Willy, the acne-faced kid on his right.

'I am pushing it,' Link said to Bartlett. 'Apologize.'

They stood for several seconds without moving.

Sue-Ellen dropped her hand from Sid's arm and moved slightly behind him. Emma slid to stand behind Link.

Bartlett stepped back. He held his palms up to Link. 'Sure.' He turned to Sue-Ellen and gave her a slight bow. He turned to Emma with the same bow. 'Ladies, if I gave you the wrong impression, I humbly apologize.' He turned away and started walking. 'Let's go, boys.'

Sue-Ellen faced Link and took a step toward him. Some of the fear still showed in her brown eyes. She offered her hand. 'It is a pleasure to meet you, Link.'

She ignored Emma.

The band stopped playing.

TWELVE

The Carp gang was holed up in a pine-board shack a mile out of Colorado City. The first week there they lay on plank beds – the one English-speaking Mexican on the floor – and groaned. The black, Idris Harris, who had just watched the horses during the robbery, found a drunken doc to sew and patch. The other two Mexicans were left gut-shot at the bank. Wesley, wounded the worst, took a .44 slug through his chest and another centered at his guts. Most other injuries had been limbs. Spike felt a bad tear in his side, plus the shoulder wound. Four bunks were pushed against walls. A table with two benches dominated the room, a rusty, wood-burning stove in the corner. Only Idris went unscathed. Spike half expected the black man to desert them.

Beginning the second week, Idris came in with an old, fat Apache woman. She carried a filthy, Indian blanket puffed full with nobody knew what, corners tied together.

Spike, with his shoulder and side pounding in pain, had his weapon in hand. 'What you bring her for?'

Idris stood in the middle of the shack. The woman went to the table and opened the blanket. She pulled tortillas and the makings of tacos from the blanket and went to work.

'You're a sorry looking bunch,' he said. 'Don't think you could gun down a kitten, let alone a man.'

Spike shifted position on the bunk, jerking with stabs of pain. The weapon stayed in his hand. He grimaced with gritted teeth. 'We got the money. We got your five-thousand.'

'I'll have to do this on my own,' Idris said.

'Take the five-thousand.'

'I already got it.'

'Ain't you gonna wait for us? Be better we hit him together.'

Idris pushed the butt of his Colt with his palm. He looked around at them as if pondering. 'Be weeks before you fellas can ride. That don't take into account drawing down and shooting. Right now, you all could be flattened by a seven-year-old girl.'

'Why the old woman?'

'The first week here told me I don't have the disposition for wet-nursing and step-and-fetch. The doc knows the old woman and she'll see to your bandages and cook and clean and look after you. The doc will come by tonight.'

'Where you going?'

'Yuma.'

Spike felt pain shoot through him again. He put his thumb on the hammer. 'You ain't thinkin' of telling Bonner the situation here?'

'You don't get that hog-leg off me, I'll send the old woman away and tell the doc you don't need him no more. You fellas are helpless. No time to be bad, mean hombres.'

Spike dropped the weapon to his side. 'You got your money, you gonna draw down on Bonner without us?'

Idris sat on one of the table benches. He snatched a piece of tortilla and popped it in his mouth. The old woman slapped his hand but not too hard. Her craggy face looked like the desert at sundown. Idris said, 'One of many possibilities I got in front of me. I'm thinking on it.' He pointed a finger at Spike. 'You better pray the hombre don't get wind of the situation here. He'd stake you and your little brother out in the mesquite and let wounds and critters and the sun have at you – after he shot you a couple more times.'

Spike laid back and tried to get a deep breath. There were a lot more things in life he didn't like than he liked. 'He won't know – 'less somebody tells him.'

Idris nodded. He eyed another tortilla. The old woman pointed her finger at him and squinted a warning. 'A stolen ten-thousand is enough to send out a posse from Gila City. By the time the bank quits telling it, it'll be twenty-thousand. They might get lucky and find you here.'

'No, they'll think we took off for Mexico, close as it is.'

'Not the way you're shot up.' He nodded to Wesley, laying quietly in the corner. 'Your little brother there might not make it.'

'He'll make it. We been through worse than this.'

'Worse?'

'Well, almost as bad.'

Idris stared at Wesley. 'Might be a month before he can sit and talk. Can you wait that long?'

'Bonner ain't going nowhere.'

Idris stood. 'He's coming after you. Newspapers got you fellas shot to pieces so he'll figure you holed up someplace. He's just got to find out where. He's a scout. You think he can't track you?'

'The trail is too cold now.'

Idris nodded. 'You're right – unless he follows the doc, or the old Apache woman, or me riding back and forth from town.'

'But you're headed for Yuma.'

'Yes, I am.' Idris crossed and opened the rickety door, allowing hot wind to blow in. He turned back to Spike. 'You better forget the woman with Bonner.'

'I don't wanna forget the woman.'

'There's no money percentage for a kidnap.'

'Maybe not, but—'

'You heard me. You're just thinking of fun. With this crew you got now, it'll be all you can handle just to dry-gulch Bonner, even after your wounds heal. You're all useless now.'

'But we got you, Harris. And you got your five-thousand. You been paid to pull down on him. Maybe we won't have to. Right now, I just want him dead. I want him to stop killing my family.'

In the corner, Wesley cried out then was still again. The old woman went to him and used a wet cloth to wipe his brow.

Idris said, 'Too much impending death in this place. I better get myself around healthy people.'

Spike tried to roll to his side but couldn't. His throat was dry and he felt pain had been with him for as long as he could remember. 'Harris, if you kill Bonner, you come back and let us know.'

Idris let the door close again. 'You quit lusting after the woman. She comes with no ransom. You better concentrate on getting better before Bonner finds you. Forget the woman.'

'I'll think about it.'

Idris opened the door again and braced against the wind. 'You might think about something else, old hoss. Every time you use that special tobacco pouch you got, think about what it cost you.'

THIRTEEN

The wedding took place the first Saturday in August, at the combination house and business in downtown Yuma. Sid Brace fidgeted nervously. Sue-Ellen Gulf flowed radiant. Link agreed to be Best Man. The daughter of the hardware store owner, Clara Swift, was Maid of Honor. Link was puzzled why Sue-Ellen had not asked Em, and why she appeared to dislike his woman. Clara was skinny, eighteen and restless for living life in a big city back east. She followed behind Sue-Ellen whom she considered worldly and well-traveled. Max and Alex attended and acted embarrassed. Alex worshipped Sue-Ellen, as he had Nellie Jo, maybe more. He looked at her at every chance, savoring her presence in the same room. Shy Max stayed in the shadows but his dark-brown eyes never left the form of the new bride. The ladies had taken over wedding and reception arrangements, not that it would be that big, maybe ten people.

With the Baptist parson and his wife in charge, the ceremony went off without a hiccup. Link stood trying to keep a smile when he felt surrounded by more people than he liked in one room. Only the presence of Emma made it tolerable. After Sid kissed the bride, Sue-Ellen turned to Link and with her hand on the back of his neck, pushed against him and gave him an open-mouth kiss that made his blood rush with a quick fever – a kiss to remember. She quickly jumped away and wrapped herself around Sid's arm and began accepting warm wishes of congratulations.

Link saw the hurt expression on Emma's face. He had to get himself outside.

Out back where the three freight wagons and stagecoach sat, Link leaned against the coach and wiped his mouth. He should have brought Em out with him. Early evening, yet the temperature had not fallen much, just no glare from the sun. Alex stomped out of the house, his square, boyish face looked about to cry. He marched past Link, shoved his hands in his pockets and turned around.

'Well, it's done now,' he said.

'They make a good couple.'

Alex stepped up to Link. 'You know what he'll be doing to her tonight?'

'They'll consummate the marriage.'

'He already had a wife. He's been married – got Nellie Jo in a family way. Now he's gonna do it again with that angel. She ain't never been with nobody, I know it.'

'Get over it, Alex.'

He pursed his lips. 'I can't. Link, I just can't. I . . . love her.'

'Well, she's very loveable.'

'Nobody loves her like me.'

'Maybe Max does.'

Alex took a step toward Link. 'Max better be careful. He's too young and dumb and obvious. He's gotta quit staring at her. She's gone from being available.'

Link said, 'She's the boss's wife now.'

Alex shook his head. 'What can I do? I got it bad.'

'You can be polite with respect – keep your feelings hid – or you can leave.'

Walking back to the house with Emma wrapped around his arm, Link reckoned they shared the same thoughts.

77

'How come she kissed me like that?' he asked.

Emma looked up at him with a knowing smile. 'You're experienced, Link. You know why.'

'But she can see I got somebody. She acts downright unfriendly to you.'

'Jealousy, my love.'

'She just got herself a new husband.'

'We'll have to see how that works out. She sure doesn't like me.'

Link stopped on the boardwalk and turned her to face him. A couple walked by, but going on Saturday night, the busiest places were the saloons. 'What if I said I about had enough stagecoach driving?'

'I can stitch and sell my quilts anywhere. Whatever you want, Link, wherever you want.'

'You're attached to that house, got a liking for it.'

'Yes, I like living there, but only because I share it with you. Without you it's just a structure. It has no life.'

He took her elbow and they continued to the house in silence. Once inside, Link glanced at the Yuma edition of the *Arizona Citizen* dropped on a chair. The two-room house had a separate bedroom with dressers and double bed. The main room contained a table with four chairs and the wood stove with shelves and cupboards, and a window that showed a view to the river. Two comfortable chairs were in front of a fireplace, the fireplace not used in the summer. Open front and back windows usually brought an evening breeze which, if not cool, at least kept the room aired. Most of their conversations took place at the dining table. Emma removed her hat and gloves. Link took off his wool jacket and hung it on the rack and went to the table with wine and whiskey.

'Pour one for you?' he asked.

'Very little.' She sat at the table and extended in a long stretch with her arms and shoulders back. Seeing his look as he watched, she smiled.

Link sat and took her hand. 'Decent wedding, as far as them things go.'

'She pines for you, Link. You got to accept that.'

'I don't and that's the end of it.' He took a swallow from the glass. 'I got to find them, Em. I got to track them down.'

'Where?'

'According to the paper, they was too shot up to head for Mexico. They's holed up someplace, not far from Gila City. They couldn't have got more'n a few miles.'

'You going to quit the stagecoach job, and go hunt for them?'

'Mebbe, I don't know.'

'What's stopping you, Link?'

'You.'

She clutched his hand to her breast. 'I can wait. You know I'll always wait.'

'I seen you hurt when Sue-Ellen planted that kiss on me.'

'It passed. I know other women will get an itch for you.'

'And men for you.'

'I repel them, you know that.'

Link pulled his hand and placed it on her cheek. 'You got to understand, Em, I ain't used to devotion like yours. I got to figure how to handle it.'

She smiled. 'You're doing fine. To your wife you were a god. I'm too mature for that. I just know you're the only man alive for me. I can live without you, but I sure don't want to.' She kissed his palm. 'Is it all right for me to talk of Yana?'

'OK. My memories of her come more about the good we had together, and mebbe I remember it better than it was.'

'Because she was so young, you were her teacher. Most of what she learned of life came from you.'

'Could be so, though she was wise in many ways. What was your life like with the major?'

She looked down at her folded hands. He had placed his hands over them. 'The major was very . . . military. I guess I'd say his entire life was stiff and strict.'

'Even with you?'

She nodded. She looked into his eyes. 'You were somewhat like that in Fort Union. You were full of killing – filled with seeking the brothers and shooting them down. But since we've been here together, I've seen a softness in your eyes – those eyes some call champagne – at least when you look at me. You move about easy, relaxed, almost Indian – but you were a scout. It confused me at first. Especially after all the cavalry and military stiffness I had known. I just couldn't reach your heart and I didn't know why. Then you rode off and after a spell, I knew I had to have you and I'd do anything.' She leaned enough to kiss his cheek. 'Maybe you don't love me, but I think you like me, more than a little.'

'Much more,' Link said.

FOURTEEN

Two days later, Link hiked to downtown Yuma. The unpainted, clapboard add-on sat back ten feet, connected to the office building. A sign on the door, Marshal, was the only announcement. Two three-foot windows with bars faced the dirt and rock road. Pine smoke curled from the rusty pipe poking up out of a lean-to roof.

Marshal Rupert Howell was in. He sat behind a makeshift desk on a makeshift chair with two empty barred cells behind him. The floor was bare, splintered wood and had not seen a broom since the end of the war. To his left a rusty, pot-belly stove glowed with pine log ends, a coffee pot perched on it. Howell spoke with his two deputies. Dressed in striped shirt-sleeves, he carried a belly pot of his own and his thick, gray hair lay perfectly brushed.

The gray eyes bore into Link with typical lawman suspicion. 'Aren't you Bonner, the stagecoach driver?'

'We talked before, Marshal.'

'Can't recall what about.' He nodded to his deputies.

They looked like twins, tall, skinny, faces unshaved and twisted and scarred, long black hair, guns low and handy – not much for conversation or greetings, they crept out the door like a pair of panthers.

Link stood to the left of the door. 'About the Carp broth-ers – I thought maybe you was in touch with the marshal in Gila City.'

'I am.'

'They got to be hiding out someplace, need tending to their gunshots.'

'They are.'

'The marshal got any idea where?'

The marshal dropped his double chin to his chest and stared at Link through his bushy eyebrows. 'Such informa-tion is law enforcement privileged. You better get yourself back to that sweet, soft dove you're living with. What she does for a dress—'

Link stiffened, his hand on the butt of his Colt. 'Marshal, talk like that will get you killed.'

He chuckled. 'My deputies are right outside.'

'They won't matter 'til after you're dead. You won't care at all.'

'Settle down, Bonner. No harm meant.'

'It was taken as such, and serious.' He took a step forward. 'You and me don't think much of each other, sow belly. You're crooked as a creek with a mind that wallows in mud. You dare to talk to me about my woman; you show no respect for her or me. I sure got no respect for you. Yuma will be a better town without you and your hired guns in it.'

The marshal looked amused, like a man in control of the world around him and all those in it – like a man dealing with a minor nuisance. 'Was there anything else you wanted, Bonner?'

When Link stepped through the batwing doors of The Trail to Ruin Saloon, he saw the black, short-brim Plains hat and Idris Harris standing at the bar. The churning anger boiling in his guts subsided immediately. He held up two fingers to

Mars the bartender and offered his hand to Idris.

Idris flashed his gleaming, white grin as he took Link's hand. 'We're a long way from Knot Head Junction, old hoss.'

'Let's get a bottle and a table.'

'Indeed, let's.'

Once seated they poured, sipped and smiled at each other.

Idris said, 'You've lost some weight.'

Link nodded. 'I have two more left, Idris.'

'I know.' He stared off for a few seconds then turned back. 'I hear tell you're with a woman.'

'Emma Fitzgerald, the same woman I knew in Fort Union.'

'It must be serious.'

'It is. How come you know what I got left?'

Idris grinned again. 'They paid me five-thousand dollars to gun you down.'

Link sat straight with a frown, the glass part way to his lips. 'Are you considering it?'

'Of course.'

Link put the glass down. 'I told you in Knot Head, I ain't no gunfighter.'

'Then I may have to reconsider.'

'Five-thousand dollars is a lot of money.'

'I'll just call it my part of the holdup cut. I held the horses. Surely that's worth five-thousand dollars.'

After a swallow, Link leaned forward. 'Do you know where they are?'

'Of course.' He poured Link's glass full, then his own. 'Only, I got to tell you, Link, I am torn between warning a one-time drinking pard what's coming, and the brotherhood of thieves.'

'You think you got some brotherhood with the Carp brothers?'

Idris stared at his whiskey glass. 'Wesley is dying – you ain't

83

getting a shot there. With the kind of care he's got, he won't last a month – maybe not the week. The slug hit him close to the heart and he needs serious surgery. The way he gargles every breath, anybody can tell he's leaking bad in his chest.'

'So, you feel loyal to Spike?'

'Come to see the true picture of it, no I don't. There's him and one Mexican might come through if Spike don't kill him. Thing is, I can't set my mind with telling you where they are. It ain't right. It might be up there with keeping your promises and riding for the brand. You get what I mean?'

'I do.'

'What I can do is give you a snippet – a nugget of information you can work around and maybe use. I can do that without really telling you where they are.'

'What will *you* do, though? I got to watch my back with you?'

Idris squinted at him. 'Spike is coming for you, old hoss. He won't be coming alone. He's got enough money to hire guns. I don't know how many. You got me beside you. Can you get anyone else?'

Link had to think. 'Most my friends are up along the northern plains. I only come down here for the Carps.' He took a sip. 'Maybe my shotgun rider, Alex, my boss, Sid – the kid, Max is too young. Em is ex-military married. She can load, and fire if she has to.'

'You got about as many friends as me.' Idris sighed. He rubbed his palm across his chin. 'Spike wants Emma. He wants her the same way he wanted your wife.'

'That ain't going to happen.'

'Can you get her out of town?'

'I can ask and I can tell her, it won't matter. She won't go.'

Idris nodded. 'If you don't get him first, I figure you got maybe three weeks to a month. He won't be riding and shooting before then. But he might send others against you.'

84

'Where? Here in town or on the stage trail or a town along the trail like he did with the dagger lady?'

'Dagger lady?'

'Lillian Bly. I think Spike Carp hired her to kill me. She tried but an Apache arrow got her.'

'Others may already be coming, Link.'

'Then I got to get him now. So, what's your nugget?'

Idris leaned back in his chair. He took his time drinking down the glass of whiskey. 'Colorado City – they got three doctors. Two are good, each with a steady practice. The third is a drunken sod. He's got an old, fat Apache woman living with him. She takes a buggy to a battered shack where she cares for some shot-up men.' He poured another glass. 'That's all I can tell you.'

'It's enough,' Link said.

FIFTEEN

Spike Carp wept real tears of sorrow when Wesley gagged his dying breath. He stood looking down at his dead brother and twisted in pain. But reality set in. He had to get out of the shack. He had never trusted the black man and was sure the scout now knew about them and was coming to wipe out the last of the Carp clan.

On the other corner bunk, the Mexican groaned. His dark eyes rolled around the room to stop on Carp – Carp sitting on a table bench, his head low, breathing quick and shallow. '*Señor, agua, por favor.* Please, *señor,* water, please.'

Carp pushed to his feet and pulled his Remington. 'If I ain't got the strength to bury my poor, dead brother, I sure as hell ain't fetching you no pump water.'

'Please, *señor.*'

Spike Carp shot the Mexican in the chest, then again through the cheek. The sound of gunfire in the small shack blocked his ears for seconds. He sat back down, smelling gunpowder and seeing white smoke around him. He shook his head, fighting for a deep breath. He had to get moving. The stagecoach driver was probably already on his way.

The effort to saddle a horse opened his side wound and he began to bleed again. He rode for Colorado City and the drunken doc. After the doc patched him, he told the doc there was no need to send the old Apache woman to the cabin any more. Everybody in it was dead. The doc said she had a few things to pick up so would make one more trip. Carp figured the 'things' were anything of value on the bodies and in the gear. He had all the bank cash – except the five-thousand the black man stole from him.

Coming out of the doc's office in glaring sunshine, Spike Carp reckoned what would set him right was a couple glasses of whiskey – no matter that it was rotgut red-eye souped up with pepper, tabasco, tobacco juice and maybe a couple spoons of kerosene in every bottle – it would put a shot of clear thinking right through his cloudy head.

He stumbled slowly through batwing doors and sat heavily in an arm chair at one of the empty tables. A girl who looked about ten, with whisker burns all over her neck, bent low for him to get a sight and took his order for a bottle and two glasses, one for her. Of the ten tables, four had old, grizzled, regular drunks and the young, restless and lazy. Two young men in their early twenties stood at the bar, dressed cowboy and a month from any kind of bath water. The bartender leaned back against a shelf of bottles in front of a bar-length mirror and stared at his shoes, a bored look on his face. He had short, black hair and a handlebar mustache. His pink shirt used wide, red garters to keep the sleeves up. Other than muted conversation, most noise came through the doors from outside – the clanging of a rolling wagon, trotting hoofs on the hard dirt road, horse tack ringing. Inside, the saloon was stifling hot with flies buzzing to cloud the door opening. The juvenile-looking girl had found richer looking game and did not join Spike Carp.

One of the young men at the bar mentioned a name that rang true with Carp. 'I'm telling you, Willy, that bastard, Link Bonner still has me to deal with. He shamed me in front of them whores they was with.'

Willy's ruddy, pink face flushed. 'That cinnamon hair sure didn't look like no whore. She looked like class. Come to think on it, Eddie, neither of them looked easy – 'cept for the men they was with. What you still chawin' on this for? That was back on the Fourth.'

Eddie slugged down to empty his glass and pounded it hard on the bar. 'The bastard needs his clock cleaned and I'm just the hombre mean enough to do it.'

Willy pushed his empty glass to the back of the bar. 'Yeah, good luck with that. I'm riding back to Yuma, want to come?'

'I ain't ready yet.'

'Stay outta trouble.' With one look around the saloon, Willy walked easy through the doors.

Eddie doubled his fist, as if still pulsing with hate. He pounded it hard and spun around with his elbows propped behind him. 'My name is Eddie Bartlett!' he shouted. 'I'm the meanest bastard in two counties! I brush my teeth with gunpowder and chew up horseshoes for breakfast and spit out nails! I can outdraw and outfight any man alive. I'm so mean nobody can take me. Don't nobody even try!' He lurched as he looked around the room. 'Anybody? Any of you jaspers want to try?'

The bartender slid a single-shot, long-barreled twelve out from under the bar and shoved it hard against Eddie's back. 'How'd you like to chew on some buckshot, loud-mouth?'

Eddie blinked as if he didn't remember where he was. 'Didn't mean nothin' by it,' he said meekly.

The bartender pulled back the shotgun. 'Settle down and settle quiet or you're done drinking whiskey in here.'

Spike Carp held up his hand to Eddie Bartlett and motioned the young lad over. Eddie staggered to the table but did not sit.

'Join me,' Carp said.

'What for?'

'I heard you mention Link Bonner. Mebbe I got some money you can earn.'

Eddie stood tall with a wrinkled face of interest. 'Okay.' He sat and watched both glasses filled. He slugged down the drink and put his elbows on the table and stared at Carp. 'I'm listenin'.'

'I had a run-in with Bonner myself.'

'Ain't that fascinatin'. Get to the money part.'

'How'd you like to do more than beat Bonner to a pulp?'

'What I'd like to do is spray his head with lead then help myself to that sweet-faced woman he's with.'

Spike Carp spread Union cash on the table. In a low voice he said, 'I'll pay you one-thousand dollars to gun the man down.'

Eddie sat stiff with raised eyebrows. 'I sure as hell see you got it. When you want it done?'

Carp cupped his chin and looked toward the doors. He felt a stitch in his chest when he thought he saw a lawman's badge pass by. What if the badge came in? He looked back at the lad. 'That's the thing, Eddie. I got to be with you, and I'm too shot up right now. I need to get better healed. Can you be in Yuma and ready so I can let you know?'

'Did he shoot you?'

'Another *hombre*.' Spike smiled, thought again. 'Yeah, Bonner dry-gulched me on the trail, left me for dead.'

'I figured him to be the type. He come up to me with his Colt already drawn. Yeah, he's that kind of back-shooter.'

'Killed my brothers too – murdered them in a horrible way. Gutted my youngest and dangled him from a Sycamore.'

'And jumped you on the trail. You know where he is.'

'Round about.'

'What about the woman?'

'I want the woman.'

'I don't mind sharing.'

Carp conjured a sour image of Emma being shared with this mud-hole swimmer. 'Well, we can dicker about that later, though I done some sharing myself in the past, but just with my brothers. Do you know the marshal there in Yuma?'

'The new one – Rupert Howell? Nope. But I know one of his deputies – Buck Davoe. When I was sixteen he was twenty-three. We run together along the outlaw trail – a little rustling, a couple stage-coach holdups, solo wagons, nothing big. He was too mean for me so I split out on my own. I mean it was bad enough us robbing the folks without him hurting them like that – 'specially the women.'

'Who's the other deputy?'

'Shipley Dupes. Don't know him too good.'

'I'd like to meet them. Mostly I'd like to meet the marshal.'

'How come?'

'I want the marshal with us when we go after Bonner. I hear-tell he's no stranger to cash payment offers. And he's no friend to the stagecoach driver. But first I want the deputies to pay Bonner some attention. Work him over to tenderize him for what's coming.'

'We all gonna have the woman?'

'Not so's anyone would notice – 'cept maybe her.'

'When do I get the thousand?'

'When I'm standing there spitting on the body of Link Bonner.'

SIXTEEN

The second day of September, Link installed wheel bearings smeared with gooey grease and tar on the propped freight wagon. Sid had chosen it for the drive to Tucson. It was the sturdiest of the three. Sid was in town to drum up stagecoach and freight business. The boys hauled a wagon of freight to horse-switch station rest stops outside Gila City and the mining town of Clinton. About noon, the air was still and hot.

In search of Carp, Link had ridden to Colorado City and found the doc's office. He even followed the old Apache woman out to the shack. The men inside were dead – including Wesley – and brother Spike had cut a trail. Idris had said the outlaw needed a few weeks to heal. Link had to be ready.

As he cleaned bearing tar and grease from his hands with turpentine then water, Sue-Ellen came from the house, wearing a dark shawl around her shoulders. The blue dress showed more bare throat than it should have. Her big, brown eyes lounged along Link.

'Link, I have coffee ready. Would y'all like a cup?'

'Yes'm.'

'Come in when ready.' Her chestnut hair flowed shiny, cheeks flushed while she stood straight, her shoulders back. She looked like what she was, a sweet-faced Southern Belle, aware that she was young, beautiful and feminine.

Wiping his hands, Link followed her into the small kitchen. A table the size of a wagon wheel dominated the center, built with wood pegs and logs brought in by wagon from the wooded hills. Two counters angled off a wall corner, one with sink and big, water hand pump, the other with shelves of food packages. The deep, ground cool room was outside the back door, forty feet away from the outhouse. A crackling fireplace with medium flame had a heavy pot of stew hanging above it. Other pans and pots hung from handles along the walls and next to an open window. He smelled lamb in the stew, and the bread she had baked that morning, and her. Her scent hung wispy like honeysuckle in the air as she sat to his right. The kitchen felt close and hot.

Link looked over at the covered bread loaf, butter and jar of peach jelly. 'Looks good,' he said.

Sue-Ellen beamed with a smile that appeared child-like. 'Do you realize this is the first time we've been alone together?'

'Yes'm.'

She smiled. 'Do you remember the wedding kiss?'

'Yes'm, though I work to forget it.'

She put her hand on his. 'I admire you, sir.' She leaned forward showing a little more than bare throat. 'Link, I have to tell you about my feelings.'

'No, you don't.'

'I must. Sid is a wonderful man. I respect the kind of business he's trying to build, but marriage hasn't turned out as I expected. I thought it would be. . . .'

'Be what?'

'More satisfying – I thought I'd be happier, feel more complete. Do you know what I mean?'

Link slid his hand out from under hers. 'Give it time. Maybe you got to grow into something like marriage. But, don't look to me, ma'am. I was married to a Pawnee girl. That ain't nothing like hooking up with a white woman. I ain't never been properly married, like in a church with a preacher and such.'

'You're with Emma, and she seems happy and satisfied. Apparently living in sin agrees with her.'

'You don't think much of her 'cause she's with me?'

'I did consider her fallen. Living with a man out of wedlock is wrong in every Christian way. Now I doubt that kind of thinking.' Sue-Ellen sliced the warm bread.

'That why you treat her so bad?' Link asked.

'I'm sorry you think that. But, I don't want to talk about Emma.'

' 'Course not.'

'I'm sure you've been with many other women.' The bread sliced, she put the knife down and looked down at her coffee cup without touching it. 'It's two more weeks 'til school starts. I wake in the morning and I feel this tension, this sense of being unfulfilled.' She put her hand on his arm. 'You're a real man, Link. I see it. I see how the boys – and even Sid – admire you. I see how Emma gazes at you with so much softness in her eyes. I know you could make a girl feel like a woman.' She leaned further toward him. 'Do I look inviting to you?'

Link sat straight on the chair. 'Don't be thinking like this, girl. You got no business.' He wanted a slice of that oven bread, with melting butter and jelly on it.

She looked straight at his eyes to draw his gaze back to her. 'I see the way you and the boys look at me.'

'Not me.'

'Alex then. I know what he's thinking. Don't tell me you haven't thought about it.'

'Before Emma, I mighta thought about it. Ain't nothing different about me, I'm just a man, but any yearnings I got in those days I used up with another kind of woman.'

'You mean those soiled doves upstairs in saloons? Yes, I hear things. Clara watches them from the hardware store. You saying you'd prefer one of those to—'

'I prefer Emma, and just Emma. You're frustrated and bored and looking for excitement – maybe even a little trouble. But you're married. You got a husband.'

She blinked, her eyes misty. 'But, Link. I'm not satisfied.'

'Work harder at it.'

'I'm willing to work hard with the right man, a real man. But he has to show some knowledge, some gentle compassion, some experience. I don't know what to do. I have no experience. I can't believe this is all I should expect, that there isn't more. My emotion just builds and builds and builds and I need release. Before we were married, when he was sweet, kissing me and pawing me, I thought about letting him do what he wanted. A few women do. Like Emma. I know now I should have. I never should have waited. If I'd found out then how little he really knew, I . . . never would have married him. I know you have that experience. With you—'

'Ain't gonna happen, lady.' He had a slice of bread. He buttered it and smeared a thick layer of peach jelly over the butter. He pointed the knife at her. 'And it don't help you being mean to Emma. She was a widow when I met her. That's different than an innocent girl don't know nothing. All she got is an interest in me. You push against her and you're pushing me. You want to talk open how you feel, you talk to your husband, not me.'

'His last wife left him, didn't she?'

'Yes'm, but she had weird notions not connected to him. I think she would've left any man.' He chomped a big bite out of the bread, savoring the tangy, peachy taste. The woman was a good bread baker and jelly maker.

'Not you, Link,' she said. 'I can see a woman following you, like Emma, but not leaving you.'

'I ain't what you think.'

Sue-Ellen closed her eyes and sighed deeply. 'Oh, I'd love to learn.' She raised her head and aimed her wet eyes at him. 'I'd love for you to teach me. Maybe it's me. Maybe I'm not female enough, just something to be looked at – or for Alex to lust after.'

'You stay away from that boy. He don't know nothing.'

'But he's so eager.'

Link pushed to his feet. He popped the last piece of bread slice in his mouth. 'Don't go scratching every corner for what you need. I'll talk to Sid. Give the marriage a chance. Give it a little time.'

Sue-Ellen slumped in the chair. 'You go ahead and have your talk with Sid. If there's a change, I'll be grateful. But now, I know what I want.'

Link said, 'I do believe I'll have another slice of that bread for the walk.'

At the bar in The Trail to Ruin Saloon, Sid sipped his beer, looking at Link over the brim. News around town came from an article in the Yuma edition of the *Arizona Citizen*. It was about William Bonney, running heavy along the outlaw trail in New Mexico Territory, calling himself Billy the Kid. The saloon was close to full with men talking low. A plump woman laughed, underdressed and painted up. Chairs scraped. Boots stomped a rough, wooden floor. A poker game went on toward the back with chips clicking. A cowboy spit at a spittoon and missed. Glasses clinked. Smoke clouded the room.

Sid said, 'Why ain't you working on the wagon wheels?'

'Got it done,' Link said. 'I'm thinking of heading on down the trail.'

'You quitting?'

'I don't like being alone with your wife. Not when I ought to be with my Emma.'

Sid gulped another slug of beer. His ruddy, flushed face showed that the glass wasn't his first. 'Something about Sue-Ellen you don't like?'

Link had ordered whiskey. He downed it, feeling the burn along his throat. 'She's a frustrated woman. You oughta take better care of her.'

Sid stood stiff. 'What you doing telling me about my wife being frustrated? You got no place talking like that.'

'No, I ain't, but you gotta treat her nicer. When you're alone together, think more about what she wants, less about yourself. You better give her more attention or she'll go the way of Nellie Jo.'

Sid pursed his lips. 'She's my wife. She sees to my needs. That's her job. I married her for Chris'sake, kept her from being an old-maid school teacher. She oughta be grateful. And you got no business messing in my married life.'

Link banged the empty glass on the bar. 'Way that woman looks she'd never be an old maid. And, you're right – ain't none of my concern. I got my own business with my own woman. Thing is, any man really looking can see Sue-Ellen is unhappy. I'm telling you, *any* man looking. But you're right. I oughta stay out of it. Not even say what I said already. And I will. I just come to town to tell you, the bearings is greased and the wagon is ready.'

'Are you taking it to Tucson?'

'I don't want to leave Emma alone for a coupla weeks. You take it.'

'I'm trying to get passengers for the stage before Butterfield and Wells, Fargo plows me under.'

Link had another whiskey in front of him. He looked at Sid's beer. 'I can see that.'

'You work for me, Link. You just make that your concern, nothing else.'

The two men turned silent. Link figured, finish out the year then move on. Stay away from the wife. Hunt down and shoot Spike Carp wherever he is. Try to stick with it 'til the end of the year, about Christmas, then be gone. Take Emma and move back up to the northern plains – maybe into Wyoming Territory or the Dakotas – someplace not so hot where skin-burning hard wind didn't blow day and night. His big questions were, could he find Carp and could he stick it out until the end of the year? He wouldn't have to. If Sid's domestic kettle started gurgling, saddle up and ride on – in six months, one month, or the day after tomorrow.

SEVENTEEN

The third weekend of September, Link drove the four-team stage out of Mineral City with Alex riding shotgun, rolling south to Yuma. Sid Brace was driving a load of freight to Cathedral City and might make it home the next day or day after. The other young one, Max hung back at the station in case freight was needed down the road. The boys were both nineteen, though Max was the most juvenile. He had a lot of growing to do with his bib overalls and bucktooth smile, but like Alex, he adored the only woman at the station, Sue-Ellen Brace.

Link hadn't spent much time there lately. He hauled freight or drove the stage to and from Mineral City, and he rode trail around Yuma and Cathedral City in search of Carp. Sid appeared full of tension and acted nervous and short-tempered. His arguments with Sue-Ellen carried to the coach and freight yard, rising in volume but not enough to make out words, except it looked like the wife withheld intimate affection from her husband. Sid took the freight job because, as he told Link, he needed time away from his wife.

Link thought that was dangerous thinking.

The stagecoach rumbled and rolled and bounced south along the rough, rocky road as the afternoon wind blew to kick up the landscape. Passengers were a plain-looking mail-order bride headed for her husband-to-be who owned an orchard in central California, a doctor well over sixty who carried a love affair with the whiskey bottle and listed his destination as Yuma, and a fragile-looking woman from Saint Louis on her way to be with her Captain in the cavalry stationed at Fort Yuma. Once in Yuma, they would connect with train or ferry to continue, or in the case of the doctor stay in Yuma.

Alex was open and friendly with the two quiet women. They paid him little attention with his bowler and straight, blond hair sticking out. Except for the hat, Alex dressed western, and as he had toward Nellie Jo, he did not hide his obvious affection for Sid Brace's wife, Sue-Ellen. Max, however, hid everything, which made him more unpredictable.

With Mineral City behind them, the stage swayed along carrying the noise of gear and luggage. Link saw five Apache tracking the stage about a quarter-mile out. He had met cavalry patrols before. Renegade Apache were always jumping reservations. He wanted to see a patrol now to move this band along. But he continued on seeing only mesquite, rocks and sagebrush, and the Apache.

No patrol came, but a single rider galloped from a mesa off to the southeast. Link kept the teams pulling the wagon while he watched. The Apache watched too. They began to drift away. The rider wore buckskin and carried his carbine loose in his hand. He swayed easy in the saddle with the stretched-leg motion of the mount like he'd been born and raised there. He had been moving in the direction of the five Apache, but now he swung toward the stagecoach without breaking his stride. Link had him as a cavalry patrol scout. As he rode closer he showed a clean-shaven face, in his late thirties, a tan Plains hat with feathers around the brim, and pitch-black hair flowing out in the wind from his shoulders.

Link began to pull back on the reins.

With one last look at the retreating Apache, the scout trotted to the stage and halted next to Link. He touched the brim of his hat, 'Gents.'

'You were riding hard,' Link said.

'Got some runaways. The patrol is an hour behind me.' He stood in the stirrups and offered his hand. 'Name is Pecos Hobbs from down south Texas way. Folks just call me Pecos. Scouting out of Fort Yuma for the soldier boys.'

Link nodded. 'Link Bonner, riding shotgun here is Alex.'

Pecos turned to watch the small band ride toward a small canyon. 'The boys in blue will be along.' He shoved the carbine in its saddle scabbard. 'A small band like them hit a family wagon twenty miles back. Killed them all, man, woman, two boys.'

The doc poked his white head out the window. 'Can anything be done, I'm a doctor.'

'They're beyond all that now, doc.' He tipped his hat looking in. 'Ladies.' He looked up at Link. 'You're the only stagecoach along this line.'

' 'Cause nobody else will touch it,' Link said.

Pecos squinted in the direction he had come. 'I see the dust cloud. Looks like I'll have company soon. We'll have a set-to with that band.' He grinned at Link. 'We bump into each other in Yuma, I'll buy you a drink.'

'Better than that,' Link said. 'I'll have my woman fix us supper.'

'Look forward to it, Link.' He nodded. 'Alex.' He bent slightly to the coach window. 'Ladies, doc. Have a safe trip.' He wheeled his big chestnut around and took off at a full gallop.

Once the coach rolled into Williamsport for the overnight stay, Link and Alex escorted the ladies to the hotel and made sure they were properly checked in. The army wife and mail-order bride were so tuckered they weren't sure they'd make it for dinner.

Link said, 'Come on, Alex. The horses are looked after. I'll buy you a meal at the hotel.'

Alex nodded. He looked up the hotel stairs where the teachers had gone.

'You can't have them all, bucko,' Link said.

'Why not?'

Once seated, they ordered a steak and potato meal washed down with coffee. Alex poured cream and sugar in his coffee and sipped.

He blinked at Link. 'I feel a restlessness in you, Link, like you ain't happy stagecoach driving no more. And like you might be expectin' somethin'.'

'Could be.' Link sat back in his chair. 'If I need you to stand with me against Apaches, can I count on you?'

'Just say the time and place.'

Link fixed Alex with a hard stare. 'What's going on in Yuma at the station?'

Alex squinted, uncomfortable. 'Don't know what you're talkin' about, Link.'

'I'm talking about the good-looking wife and you know it.'

Alex looked around the noisy room. 'Max makes it so obvious he'll get us both in trouble. He hangs around with his tongue hanging out, be hard for anybody not to notice.'

'You telling me something *is* going on with the wife?'

'A lot of something. Now with Sid outta town overnight, they are at it like a coupla bunnies.'

Link sat back while the pretty, young waitress eyed Alex as she brought plates piled with steak, fried potatoes and beans. 'You been there too?' he asked.

Alex blinked. 'Don't know what you mean, sir.'

'Say it out.'

'Yes, sir. She keeps sayin' it's wrong and we shouldn't be doin' it and stop doin' it and then she tells us how to do it so she likes it.'

'Not the both of you together?'

'No, sir. Max gets mad at me on account he wants to be the only one. I never wanted to go this far. I just wanted to hold her tight, touch her body, maybe kiss her a little.'

'Sure you did. But you kept thinking what was inside that dress, the movement, the slick, smooth skin you wanted.'

'She's so eager, so needy.'

'How dumb you think Sid is about his wife?'

'He must already think Max is up to something.'

Link shook his head while he cut steak. 'You boys – you're next to a woman with a boiling kettle below her belly and a slippery itch her husband can't scratch, and all you think about is how good it feels and how you can keep it going.'

Alex nodded. 'Pretty much, that's it.'

'What you think Sid is going to do?'

'Get real mad. Maybe fire us.'

'He fires you with a gun in his hand, you ain't never going to work nowhere again. We get back there I want you to quit. You make Max quit. I tell you, son, history is full of what you boys is doing, and it don't never end good.'

Alex shoveled in a spoonful of potatoes. 'You been there too, Link?'

'She put her hand on my arm.'

'What'd you do?'

'Moved my arm.'

EIGHTEEN

The stagecoach rolled into Yuma with two sales drummers in addition to the three passengers, picked up in Eureka and delivered to the hotel. Link and Alex continued to drive the ladies to the riverboat depot. Afterward, they rolled on into the house-station to unhitch the horses. Link just wanted a long, warm bath with Em in his arms. His body ached from stagecoach movement; the reins of the four-up team brought a painful throb to his fingers. First thing in the yard he noticed the freight wagon Sid had driven loaded with goods, now sitting empty, the back axle twisted.

The atmosphere outside the house reeked with tension right off.

'Faithless whore!' Sid shouted from inside the house.

'Mr. Brace,' Max cried. 'It ain't what you think.'

Link eased down off the stage seat. He felt a tingling across his forehead. His face flushed. He smelled recent cooking from the house – Sue-Ellen had baked bread earlier. With his tiredness, he thought of just walking on home to the house and Em. But he felt drawn to events inside. When he started for the house, Alex fell in behind him. Link turned while he loosened the rawhide loop off his Colt and pulled it. He pointed a finger at Alex. 'Unhitch the team.'

'But . . .' Alex said.

'Do as I say.'

The outside door to the kitchen was open. Link went in with his Colt pointed down along his leg, ready to cock the hammer. Nobody was in the kitchen. A sliced loaf of bread sat on the table, butter and peach jelly alongside, three slices missing.

Sid's ragged voice came from the bedroom. 'How long you two been going on?'

'Nothing is going on, Sid,' Sue-Ellen said, her voice shaky.

'Sir,' Max squeaked. 'It ain't what you think.'

'You said that. What is it then, boy?'

Link moved to the open bedroom doorway. Sid had his Colt in his hand pointed at Sue-Ellen. She clutched a red dress bunched in front of her naked body. Her beard-scraped face matched the redness of the dress. She shivered in fear. Max stood next to her wearing only his long john bottoms. His bucktooth, white face grimaced in terror. Sid turned to Link, his eyes burning coals of hatred and betrayed discovery, his expression telling Link he would never again be the man he once was. His Colt wavered between Sue-Ellen and Max.

'Stay outta this, Link,' he said, 'unless you was part of it too.' He started to swing the Colt toward Link.

'Don't,' Link said. He cocked the hammer, ready to raise his arm.

Sid paused. 'No, it wouldn't be you. You got a woman. It was them.' His face wrinkled on the verge of tears. 'I loved her, Link.' He swung the Colt back to the couple, then to Sue-Ellen. 'Whore. You ain't nothin' but a whore.'

The room blasted with the gunshot as Sid shot Sue-Ellen in the throat. Her arms flew out exposing her naked body. The dress fluffed to the floor as she fell back on the bed, both hands clutching her bleeding throat. Blood gushed from her neck to soak the sheet around her head. Max gagged and bent forward, then stumbled with shrieks and tears. He took a step to run for the door. Sid shot Max through the right temple with another deafening blast. Max's head twisted and thudded against the wall. He somersaulted and froze.

Sid swung his Colt toward Link. Link had aimed and was ready to pull the trigger. The man's face looked flushed, eyes wide and wild, spittle flicking while he blubbered and retched incoherently. He bent his elbow and pushed the muzzle in his mouth and pulled the trigger to a muffled snap of gunfire. His face puffed and his head went inside out with spray, and gray chunks spurted away to splatter against the mirror. He collapsed as if he had no bone structure, as if his clothes had fallen off a closet hook. The room smelled of burned gun-smoke and rust with white puffs in the air as Alex ran into the kitchen from outside, knocking over a chair. He froze at the open bedroom door.

'Jesus wept,' he said.

Win Trisdale, the third Yuma Deputy Marshal, who some folks thought should have been marshal, sat the kitchen table getting the story from Link and Alex. Win looked squat with his Boss Stetson, big ears and belt-draw. He wore a black and gray striped wool shirt and black pants with a dark-blue silk vest, the fresh-shined star pinned to the lapel. The fire had gone out in the fireplace. Link decided not to involve Alex as part of the wife fooling business in order to maybe allow the lad a longer life. Win got what happened and what had been going on between Max and the good-looking, itchy wife. He said he had seen Sue-Ellen on occasion and could easily understand how such foolery might come about. She had a heat that radiated from her and just naturally made some men hungry, especially the youngest of them.

The undertaker wagon hauled the bodies away.

Max's parents told Link they didn't believe for a minute

their good boy could get involved in such immoral shenanigans – he was a Christian, God-fearing lad. Their grief brought tears while they arranged a funeral for Max with church services. Link and Alex were invited.

Neither Sid Brace nor the former Sue-Ellen Gulf had kin that anybody could locate, or wanted to take the time to find. There was no will so Alex said he'd take over the stage and freight line. He and Link would run the lash-up. That was what the serious, young, bowler topped, blond-haired Alex told Link – Link shook his head.

As for Link, he reckoned he was done with the stage and wagon driving part of his life. If Spike Carp didn't make his move soon, Link would have to move for him. But he had to find the wounded outlaw first.

Four days after the funeral, Link had breakfast with Alex, ham and eggs with fried chips and three cups of coffee. Emma was entertaining a quilt buyer with coffee and blueberry biscuits at the house. Link hankered for her blueberry biscuits.

In his short time as business tycoon, Alex looked a little older and less happy with corporate responsibility. The hotel café had couples mostly, with several single gents who were staying there. Since Alex was young and randy, he spent some time studying the girls and women dining together or with their men. Pottery thudded, silverware rattled, pots and pans clanged over a background of muffled voices. Girls under twenty scooted between tables taking and delivering orders, their young, girlish voices sounding like church-bells during a gunfight. Alex's stares lingered longer with them.

Some men waited at the open doorway to the hotel lobby for tables to come free. Talk between other men was mostly what to do about the Indian problem. Lakota and the Sioux rode on murdering raids up north. Many felt the Apache

were on the prod, big time. The government spoke of them
as nations with sympathy yet treated them as destitute
without rights. White people figured the government might
eventually come up with a solution to the Indian issue, if they
hadn't already – just most folks didn't know about it. Leave
that sort of thing to the army and those politicians back east.

Alex sipped coffee, said, 'I hadn't figured on all the paperwork, all the danged bookkeeping. And I can't read so good.'

'Who handles paperwork?' Link asked.

'My ma. She had schoolin'. Me and Pa had none. I picked
up some readin' words but not enough to run a business. I
see an end to all this head work scribblin'.' He grinned and
forked in a piece of ham. 'What the hey, Butterfield gonna
run us out of business anyways. 'Tween them and Wells,
Fargo, little operations got no chance. Maybe I ought to go
to work for them.'

'What *will* you do?'

'Well, I got me a shotgun rider, an orphan, seventeen,
wears bib overalls like Max did, and got blond hair down to
his tail-bone. He's a real sharpshooter, and can handle a four-
up 'most as good as you, Link. And he can read, went to a
missionary school to learn his words and numbers. He's out
in the lean-to at the barn where you used to sleep – name of
Jason. That's biblical, ain't it?'

'Far as I know. You should remember from praying with
Nellie Jo.'

Alex wiped his plate with toast, nodding, looking wistful.
'Yeah, Nellie Jo.'

'You taking Jason on as a partner?'

'No, I'm giving him the whole lash-up. I got to move on,
Link. I'm dang near twenty, old enough, should leave home
anyway. Maybe get on a cattle drive 'fore they all get fenced
out. Maybe look for gold up in the Dakotas. I'll be like you
was before Emma, and become a scout – or just drift. You

been a lot of places.'

Link nodded, staring at his coffee cup. There wasn't time to remember all the towns and trails and people and gunfights. 'Yep, a lot of places,' he said.

Alex said, 'Looks like I'll be rolling out before noon with Jason shotgun.'

Link sat straight. 'Emma and I are planning a picnic upriver, maybe Sunday. We're coming into October and Idris says Spike Carp might be close to healed. I don't know who he hired or how or from where they'll hit me. I got to talk to Emma about what to do when they come. I want to count on you but it won't work if you're up in Mineral City or parts between.'

Alex turned ashen. 'Link, I got stage runs. You think it might be soon?'

'I expect it any day.'

'Maybe I ought to take a couple weeks off from the run, or let Jason take 'em.'

'That's up to you, Alex.'

Alex nodded. He squinted at Link. 'You ever think about Sid?'

Link put egg on his ham and pushed it in his mouth. The taste didn't come close to Emma's breakfast. It seemed no matter what a man's needs, Emma just did it better. Somehow, thinking that made him feel guilty. Yana had been a girl. Link was now with a woman. And he knew the difference. The guilt over Yana joined what he felt about Sid Brace. 'I got guilt about Sid. In the saloon I told him he ought to take better care of his wife. I never should have said that to him. Could be he just didn't know about women. He didn't know what they needed or how to provide it. He was a good man, just unlucky with wives.'

Alex nodded. 'She said she wanted to tell him. She coulda told him what she needed but he didn't listen.'

'You and Max sure did, didn't you?'

'Link, I'd done anything and everything she wanted. I sorta got lost in her. But Max didn't even keep being hisself. He was all over in love.'

'You see where it got him?'

Alex shook his head. 'Sad. How many women you figure walking around like her, so much need, not gettin' what she really has to have?'

NINETEEN

The first Sunday in October 1876, Link Bonner loaded the blanket and picnic basket in the back of the Studebaker buckboard – the wagon painted blue with black wheels. Emma's palomino and his old chestnut hitched, the mares standing patiently. He slid his new '76 Winchester rifle behind the bench seat. The sun was at noon, the air still, enough snap for coats and a buffalo cover on their laps.

Link could not see downtown Yuma from the house. Cottonwood, willow, juniper and mesquite growth – plus an abundance of rocks – surrounded the house except for a narrow path and clearing along the river about thirty yards away. He looked in that direction anyway. Now and then a flutter rushed across his chest. So many places perfect for ambush. A smell of fish came from the slow-moving river. Insects provided a sparse web cloud between water reflection and sunshine with a soft hiss. Sparrows fluttered back and forth nipping at the cloud. The caw of black crows called each other from tree branches along the river. East, beyond the house stretched scrub grass and rocks, the land flat to jagged cliff-front mesas and arroyos to rocky, rolling hills in the distance and mountains beyond. He pulled on his leather gloves while he waited for her, and squinted in the direction of downtown Yuma. For an unknown reason he placed his hand on the walnut grip of his Colt .45 Peacemaker and held it there.

When he heard footsteps along the path, he eased the rawhide loop off the Colt hammer.

'Kinda jumpy, ain't you, Link?' Idris said.

'Good reason,' Link said.

Idris walked the path with Win Trisdale, the third Yuma deputy – Win's short, stumpy legs barely able to keep his squat frame alongside slim, long-legged Idris – his Montana peak Stetson low above his eyes. Idris grinned as they came up, the two scars on his black cheek raised up. He had a thin gambler's mustache and wore his dark Plains hat low.

Link shook their hands as Emma came from the house in a gray dress with a neck scoop and without hoop or bustle. She wore a frilly, wide-brimmed hat. Her cinnamon hair held with a hair band fell free behind her ears to just below her waist.

The visitors touched the brim of their hats.

'Gentlemen,' Emma said. She brushed against Link as she bent to put her purse next to the picnic basket, the purse made of dark-wool quilts, of course.

Win Trisdale shifted uncomfortably. He leaned toward Link. 'Mebbe we can go off someplace to talk private.'

Emma turned. She stood close to Link and fixed the deputy with her deep-indigo stare. Her full lips held a slight smile.

Link said, 'Ain't nothing going on Emma don't know about. Talk free.'

Win leaned against the wagon side, his elbow on the rail. His shiny-blue, silk vest held the deputy star, glinting brightly against the dark blue. 'I can tell you who's coming for you – the marshal and his two deputies, Buck Davoe and Shipley Dupes. I hear tell he was paid three-thousand dollars to split with his boys any way he wanted. Likely convinced them the killin' is part of their peace-keeping job and gave 'em each a five-hundred dollar bonus for doin' it. Most men know why the marshal wants you dead.' From under his Stetson he looked directly at Emma then turned his eyes away.

Link said, 'There ain't no respect between the sow belly and me.' He felt Em lean her back tight against him. 'When I seen the deputies, one of them carries twin Colts with pearl handles. I don't know his name.'

Win said, 'That'd be Buck Davoe. He's the meanest of the pair.'

'You know when they'll hit?'

Idris said, 'Waiting for word from Spike Carp. Spike's got some hot-headed kid with him, Eddie Bartlett. Talk is you had words with him and two of his pards, Willy and Woody. They might be with the kid. Come in for a coupla hundred each.'

Link frowned. 'I don't remember the kid.'

Emma said, 'Fourth of July, in front of the hotel with Sid and Sue-Ellen.'

Idris said, 'That's the polecat. He jabbered about the incident many times, figure you shamed him in front of the ladies.'

Link reckoned Em needed to be touched so he circled his arms around her waist and rested his palms on her stomach. She placed her hands over his. 'You still with Carp, Idris?' he asked.

'Not lately. I keep in touch. I guess I'm still sort of considered part of the gang. I don't know about the Mexican in the cabin with him.'

'The Mexican and Spike's brother Wesley, are dead,' Link said. 'I was at the cabin. An old Apache woman cleaned out any value. Carp had already left. He's hidin' out somewhere in or outside Colorado City.'

'Not for long, now,' Idris said.

Link lightly touched his nose to the back of Emma's hair for the scent. 'So, that's six.'

'Carp makes seven,' Win said. He pushed away from the wagon. 'Damn it, Link, I wish I could stand with you but I can't officially take sides – not if I want the marshal job.' He touched his hat brim. 'Sorry for the language, ma'am.'

Emma smiled.

'I got me, Emma, and maybe Alex. Are you still with me, Idris?'

Idris grinned again. 'I might be able to do more damage if I stay with the gang. We can hit them from two sides. Carp thinks he already paid me and I'm with him. If I stand with you in a row we make it easier for them.'

Link nodded. 'I want to hit a few first before they're ready. The weakest of the bunch is Eddie Bartlett and them shadows, Willy and Woody. I seen their eyes on the Fourth. They're all noise, got no grit.'

Win stepped back to stand beside Idris. 'They ain't showing themselves much these days. I figure they're waiting to come in with Carp.' He looked down at his boots. 'Most town people don't know what's about to happen. Them that do know don't care. Folks got their own issues and problems.'

Link squeezed Em tight. 'We sure got ours.'

Idris stepped forward. He winked at Emma then looked at Link. 'We'll get it done, old hoss.'

Along the river about a mile from the house, Link stopped the wagon. Emma sat beside him on the bench seat with her hand on his leg.

'You've been here before,' she said.

Link stepped down and offered her his hand. When she stood beside him, he said, 'We ain't got time or space for some picnic. I brought you here to show you something.'

Emma studied his face.

Link led her to the edge of the river. Tall grass grew, set around the cottonwoods and willows. A space about six feet next to the shore had been hacked clear. 'I got three waist-high logs connected and hammered deep in the mud. You see it there between the river and the flat coming in. It'll make a decent barrier for you.' He took her wrist and pulled her around the barrier to the edge of the moving water. 'Four more logs is tied together here as a kind of raft.'

Emma stood stiff. 'I know what you're saying, Link and it won't do you no good. I won't leave you.'

He took her shoulders in his hands and faced her. 'If I go down, Em, you got to leave me. If I'm dead, you got to look for yourself. Those men will—' he shut his eyes tight. 'You must get out and away.'

'I got my Whitneyville .32 revolver in my purse. I know how to use it. I can make an account of myself.'

'I know you can. But there's a bunch of them and they got more guns. When you know I'm gone, you ride yourself out here. You hide behind the barrier while they come after you. Shoot as many as you can but don't run empty. If it gets open, push off the raft and float yourself over there to California. If any of them swim after you, pick 'em off where they float. Carry spare cartridges and keep your purse close – from this time on.'

'I already do, but my purse is in the wagon.'

'I can't say about Idris and Alex. They may get hit before me. But if I go down permanent, you get yourself out here and stand them off 'til you can get in the water. You better keep your mare saddled. Ride her wherever you go, even if it's just a block. I'll do the same.'

'Then I got to quit wearing these dresses and get myself back into buckskin pants.'

'The tight pair? That'll be distracting for me.'

Emma threw her arms around his neck and pushed tight against him. 'Link, oh Link,' she cried.

'Hush up, girl. If I can pick off a couple before they all hit at once, we maybe got a chance.'

She pushed away, her deep-blue eyes liquid. 'You don't believe that. You don't think we have any chance, do you?'

They started walking back to the wagon. 'We might,' he said. 'I just want you to be ready. What you got in the basket?'

They reached the wagon and Emma got her purse strap over her shoulder. She picked up the basket, 'Fried chicken, deviled eggs, sliced tomatoes and apples. As long as we're here—'

Link heard the thump and jangle of two running horses back along the trail, coming at them. He took three steps away from Emma, the Colt in his hand and cocked.

Emma dropped the basket and began to reach into her purse. 'Link?'

'It started,' he said.

TWENTY

The two deputies galloped straight at them, Buck Davoe with one of his pearl-handled Colts in hand. He turned directly for Link, firing a wild shot. Link pulled the trigger, the bullet tore off the left ear of the horse. Shipley Dupes rode his black stallion into Emma, knocking her back against the wagon wheel. Her .32 revolver flew out of her hand. Link fired again, hitting Davoe through the arm. Davoe leaped from the saddle on to Link.

Emma crawled for the revolver while Dupes swung down from the stallion above her. The thin, scarred faces of the deputies looked determined and cruel. Link ducked and tossed the leaping Davoe over his head and aimed for Dupes who reached Emma just as she gripped her revolver. Link fired and Dupes grabbed his hip and spun around. Dupes fired at Link and missed. Davoe came up behind Link, drawing his left pearl-handled Colt.

Link felt the approach and saw a shadow. He turned to fire when a bullet from Dupes seared across his back just above waist level. Link arched with the scorching pain, swung his gun arm out and pulled the trigger. His shot missed. A rod of fire pushed against his lower spine.

Emma rolled twice along desert dirt and rock. Her dress ballooned out around her throwing dirt and sand spray. She

116

stopped and fired at Dupes, hitting him in the left hand.

Link felt the end of the Colt push against his neck. Dupes stomped a boot on Emma's hand holding the .32, pinning it to the ground. He aimed at her head.

'Stop!' Davoe shouted. 'We ain't supposed to kill you but if you keep on I'll drop you like a coyote.'

Link watched Dupes' Colt push closer to Emma's forehead, his boot still on her hand. 'I'll kill her right here where she's layin', swear to God, I will.'

Behind Link, Buck Davoe said, 'Drop the hog leg.'

Link jammed his elbow back into Davoe's wounded arm, dropped to his knee and aiming back between his legs, shot Davoe through the boot. Dupes aimed away from Emma, directly at Link. Just as he fired, Emma rolled to her right and punched his leg with her left fist to throw off his aim. The bullet kicked up dirt at Link's right heel.

In a snap of cracking gunfire, Link shot Dupes through the waist, making him leap sideways and backward, his left hand gripping the wound. With her gun hand free, Emma shot Dupes, chipping away part of his left ear. She fired again, hitting him through the chest.

Davoe had grabbed his foot with both hands and rolled away. He clutched one of his dropped Colts and turned to fire. By then, Link had brought his aim around and shot Davoe, tearing off his nose. He cocked again then stood and shot Davoe through the left eye, and again through the heart.

Emma was on her knees panting, staring at Dupes who staggered as he struggled to breathe, his weapon dropped. Link stumbled over to her and shot Dupes through the heart.

Link fell on his back close to Emma, breathing fast, his heart racing, his back aflame, burning in pain, his hands shaking. Lying on his back kept pressure against the wound. Emma crawled to him, sniffling, her chin quivering. Tears

117

flowed down her cheeks. Her hands trembled and she dropped the revolver. She slid her arms across his chest and laid her head between them as she shuddered. He gently placed his hand on the side of her face.

'We're alive,' she whispered as if surprised. 'God, we're still living.'

'They ain't,' Link said. 'We cut 'em down by two.'

After Emma and Link pushed the bodies into the river, they sat on the blanket next to the wagon. It took most of an hour for them to settle down. Emma looked over Link's back. She told him the skin had torn in a thin, ragged line but by wrapping him with her petticoat, she'd stopped most of the bleeding.

'I get you home I'll wrap it proper,' she said. 'We can tighten it closed with sticky, bandage tape.'

For another half-hour they sat in silence. Emma stared at the black wagon wheel, Link at the hem of her gray dress. What he thought of was how close she'd come to getting hit. Any different twist of the action, they both might have died. He had to think of what else was coming. He felt himself outside life, in an unreal world of what just happened, beyond the comfort of normal living.

It wasn't like when he shot the Carp brothers or Indians in battle – or robbers and killers he had slain. Then, it had been concern over his own life and how to keep it alive, at times driven by hate or revenge. Now he felt fear, a mind-numbing dread some bullet might find its way into Em. When he had watched Yana suffer from the Carp brothers – yes, he had felt hate. But he knew with everything inside him, she would die, and after, he would die. That was a known. But he didn't die, he healed, and that left only revenge, and the vengeance came close to getting done – as soon as he got rid of the crowd surrounding it.

Emma broke the silence. 'The marshal might not be far behind.'

'I don't think so,' Link said. 'Davoe said they weren't supposed to kill us. They was sent to soften me up and have at you before the others hit us. With you defiled, I'd be blood red mad and out of my head and do a string of dumb things to make it easier for them.'

Emma narrowed her indigo stare at him. 'If they try anything like that, I won't wilt, Link. I won't plead and whimper and beg them to stop – they'll pay no attention to that kind of drivel. As long as I have my Whitneyville in hand, any man who tries me will get a hot thirty-two caliber somewhere through him. If they hit me and take my pistol,' – she reached in her purse – 'I have this here short-blade Bowie ready to amputate his manhood.' She showed a shiny Bowie knife with a blade about six inches, the crescent-moon tip sharpened on both edges and along the back to about an inch to cut on the backswing, then serrated to the handle so it tore and chewed coming out.

He had seen them during the war, and up along the northern prairie, some with blades twelve inches long, carried in a sheath like a pistol. No way around it, a knife fight between men was the bloodiest kind of skirmish.

'I'll bet you can use it,' Link said.

'I did, at times when the major and his troops were attacked by hostiles, or when the fort or our camp was invaded and women taken. I had to protect myself and what was mine.'

Link shook his head. 'You ain't no delicate flower all the time, are you, Emma Fitzgerald?'

She smiled sweetly, putting the Bowie back in her purse. 'Only for you, my love.' She leaned to him and gave him a warm, wet kiss. 'You think we're settled enough for some fried chicken and deviled eggs?'

'Yes'm. Mebbe we ought to reload first.'

Driving the buckboard back to the house, Link eyed the trail brush and outlying desert closely. His back ached. He put his hand on Emma's leg. 'I'll unhitch the horses and saddle them. You clear the floor inside the house in case we got to defend there.'

'You think they'll come this soon?'

'They might wait 'til dark – or the sow belly marshal, Rupert Howell might try on his own. By now, somebody found the bodies floating by.'

'He can't be arrogant enough to think he can take you alone.'

Link smiled at her. The woman just kept squirming herself deeper in his heart. He said, 'With you beside me toting that thirty-two pop-gun and lethal sow belly sticker, we ain't nobody to fool with.'

'We have more than a good chance to come out of this.' She hugged his arm. 'Tell me you believe that.'

'Now we got the odds narrowed a bit – I hope the marshal does try something on his own. That ain't his personality, or what little character he carries. He'll likely have back shooters along for the fun.'

'We stick together, Link. If I'm going to die, I got to be touching you.'

'We better think about living and what we do after this.'

Emma squinted against a setting sun. 'You just head on out, Lincoln Bonner, I'll be sitting right next to you.'

'Wherever?'

'Whatever direction you point the buckboard.'

Link thought again what had been on his mind for a bit. 'You like me well enough to want to marry up with me, Emma Fitzgerald?'

She leaned heavily against his arm. 'I think we better.'

Link peered sideways at her. 'Because.. . .'

'Because, Lincoln, I've been carrying your child more'n two months now.'

TWENTY-ONE

In the line shack three miles southwest of Colorado City, Spike Carp used the silver-paper, peeled mirror to practice his draw. His side still had some dull pain but the shoulder worked well enough. He was ready and he had enough help.

The ranch where the shack stood was abandoned, the owners eventually learning that the southwest desert burned hostile and deadly for men, women and cattle alike. Texas longhorns hadn't run on the land in five years or more. When a man lost his children first, then his wife, there was no reason to go on. Some tried again at another place farther north where there was water. A few found a new wife, maybe younger to last longer, and to bear more children. Others gave up on ranch life to become drunks or ride the outlaw trail.

The Carp family had chosen the outlaw life.

Spike Carp remembered his daddy leaving Arizona to try again just out of El Paso. He went bust there after having a house full of boys that drained his young, replacement wife of all hope and breath. Daddy just rode off – no by your leave or good-bye. At eighteen, Spike Carp had the five young boys to feed and raise. He often thought of following along his daddy's trail. Other than chopping wood and working a place more farm than ranch – with two longhorn steers and

122

one cow – he had no life skills. But he practised his draw and could shoot straight, and figured he felt no bother to blast a man dead front or back, or force his way on a woman for his pleasure.

A political war was starting to split the nation. It held no concern for him. Once he became part of the war he fell in with others of his kind and found he was well-suited to the rob and kill and rape kind of life. He had to abandon his youngest brothers until they grew some but they all got together again long after the war ended – until they wanted to have some fun with a young Pawnee squaw and brought all the doom and damnation of hell down on them.

Spike Carp heard three horses riding up. He stepped to the open doorway and watched them coming. His Colt Peacemaker, cleaned and well oiled, slipped in and out of the holster slicker than syrup from the bottle. His cartridge belt held a full load of .45s. He thought about a rifle but he wanted to be close to the polecat – close enough to watch his eyes when he died – close enough for his woman to see – before Spike helped himself to her flirtatious charms. Maybe the stagecoach driver should be made to watch again, as he had with his wife, before he was shot to pieces. Afterward, those riding with Spike had to be taken care of, no longer needed, no sense letting them live. The two problems might be Idris Harris and the marshal, Rupert Howell. The deputies could be back shot. The kid, Eddie Bartlett and his baby sidekicks, Willy and Woody presented no problem. They showed spunk but not much backbone. Most important, Spike had to kill Bonner first. If the deputies already had fun with Emma, Spike still wanted her. He would take his revenge on the ex-scout for his brothers through her.

The three riders – Eddie Bartlett with Willy and Woody – Bartlett looking cocksure with his ancient, Navy cross-draw .36, Willy and Woody, close like brothers. Willy, blond and green eyed, Woody, black-eyed with some Mexican blood, neither yet twenty – reined in front of the rickety shack doorway, puffing clouds of sand and dirt. Bartlett looked anxious, eager with news. Spike waited for whatever update they brought. The boys swung down as Spike watched them from the doorway. Their horses snorted dust and shook their heads as the boys tied them to a log rail next to the half-empty trough. The rail looked splintered and half eaten through with wear. Eventually, the wind blew the grit away.

'Well?' he said.

Eddie Bartlett pulled his black Plains hat and pounded it against his torso to puff away some trail dust. 'We been cut down by two, Spike.'

'The deputies?' Spike said.

'A coupla boys fishin' seen the two bodies flowin' down-river and set up a holler. The deputies was pulled out, shot something ragged, deader'n pan fried fish.'

Spike pulled his hat brim low and peered off to the horizon. 'Anybody see if the scout or his woman was hit?'

'No way of knowing,' Willy said.

'Is the third deputy – what's his name?'

Bartlett pulled his canteen from saddle and took a slug. 'Win Trisdale.'

Spike nodded. 'Trisdale – short, stumpy *hombre*, wants to be marshal. Has he joined Bonner's gang?'

'He rode on out to Gila City. Him and the marshal there is tight, maybe talk about the holdup, maybe just jaw and sip, dunno.'

Spike was sure he saw something out there. 'Rider on the horizon. Did you let somebody follow you? You boys get your horses away from the cabin. Too many on that worn rail anyways. Take mine with you.'

The boys untied the horses and led them around behind the shack to an old, broken, clothesline post where they retied them. They came back looking at the same spot in the distance as Spike.

Woody pulled his stained, white, Montana Peak Stetson and leaned forward, squinting. 'It's the black, riding this way. Can't miss that white stallion.'

Spike said, 'I always liked that big, white albino of his.'

They stood in silence, watching Idris Harris ride toward them, his image still wavy against the backdrop of distant mountains.

Eddie Bartlett said, 'Is he still with us, you think?'

Spike doubled his fists, irritated. He glared at the others. 'Now, how come he knows about this place and we're here? It's more than him just following.'

'I told him,' Willy said. He shrugged and poked his boot toe in the dirt and sand, paying attention to the grooves he made. 'Spike, he had part of your holdup money to gun down the scout. I figured he was still part of us, still going in with us to kill Bonner. I told him where we was.'

Spike had his hand on the butt of his holstered Colt. He had an idea and relaxed. 'What's done is done. You boys let the black ride on in. After him and me have some short howdy-do, and he mounts up to leave, you don't let the black ride out. You understand. We ride out. He stays.'

'We got you,' Bartlett said. 'But ain't we gonna need him?'

'Not if he went to the other side,' Spike said. 'He's taking too long to make his move, and I think he switched. He knows the scout from a time before.'

The boys spread in a line when Idris Harris rode in, his black face shiny with trail sweat. He glanced at them with a nod, then looked at Spike, standing in the doorway.

'Idris,' Spike said. 'Come in and sit. I got coffee. You come to tell me Bonner is dead and his woman is weeping and carrying on now she got no man attention? And she does need man attention.'

Idris swung down from his albino stallion, glanced at the three standing men, and followed Spike into the shack. 'No, I come to warn you he's got help. I'm not staying.'

'Like that shotgun rider, Alex?'

'And I think one other, not sure who.'

They sat in wooden armchairs at a stained, unpainted and splintered table while Spike poured coffee. The pot sat on a rusty stove. A kerosene lantern was the only other object on the table. Two bunks were pushed against the thin, weather-worn walls. The youngest two slept on the tobacco-spit-stained floor. Empty whiskey bottles, cigarette butts, old newspapers, and clothes littered the floor. Cold weather coats hung from the walls.

Spike used his special tobacco pouch to sprinkle tobacco on corn-husk paper for a roll-your-own. He said, 'Mebbe it's the wanna-be marshal, the short, stubby one.'

Idris studied the pouch. 'Could be. How's the healing coming along?'

Spike bounced the pouch lightly on his palm as if fondling it. He pocketed the pouch and lit the cigarette. 'I'm about ready, any day now. What are *you* waiting for?'

Idris took one sip of coffee and set it down on the table, wrinkling his nose in distaste. He looked around the inside of the shack, then out the open doorway. 'You heard about the deputies?'

'The boys just told me. We figure first off to kill the shotgun rider. Then we burn that little house of hers down around them, flush 'em out so we can pick him off. What you hear from Rupert, the marshal?'

'Nothing.' He put both hands on his knees and leaned forward. 'Well, I just came out to give you news about the deputies, and the boy helping Bonner.'

'You ain't gonna ride in with us?'

'I'll try to at least wound him before you get there. When

126

you figure to go?'

'Today or tomorrow. Seems like a long ride jes' for a short visit.'

'I came to pass information, not to visit. We can meet up in town.'

'Whatever you say, Idris.'

Spike saw a change in Idris' dark eyes when he said that, as if it came out phony, suspicious. He hoped he wouldn't have to draw down on the gunfighter. The boys might get him eventually, but Spike knew he'd already be dead. The men rose together. Spike followed Idris to the door. The boys stood placed at points of a triangle around the albino, looking at Idris with youthful grins. Standing by his saddle, Idris eyed each one in turn. Spike watched him pull his canteen and take a swallow.

Bartlett, standing off to the right said, 'You have yourself a nice ride back, Idris. We'll be seeing you in Yuma.'

Spike saw that as Idris lifted his left leg to the stirrup, he unhooked the rawhide strap to his Colt hammer. The albino shifted and snorted with the weight as Idris eased his right leg around.

'Not yet,' Spike whispered low under noise cover from the rig and the albino stomping. 'He can still use the horse for cover. Wait. Wait.'

When Idris swung his right boot down into the stirrup to sit in the saddle, he drew his Colt as the three boys, already pulled, dropped to one knee below any crossfire and began to shoot. Idris fired one shot that chipped the wood above Spike's head, making him duck slightly and move partly beside the doorway for cover. Clipped, cracking gunfire split the desert air. Idris jerked and jumped in the saddle while bullets slammed into his body from three directions – a bullet tore through his neck, another went into his ear. The albino stallion reared and jumped and screamed as bullets hammered into rider and horse. Five shots hit the horse making him stop still, shiver, and droop his head. The albino dropped to its forelocks and stayed, quick breaths from his big nostrils blowing against the sand, puffing dirt, not yet toppling. Idris' Plains hat tipped forward and fell from his head. The pistol dropped out of his hand to the ground billowing a small cloud of dust as it landed. In seconds, the boys had fired out. The two youngsters each clicked once against empty chambers. After the repeated snap of shots, white gunsmoke blew away in the silent breeze. The boys stood without stepping, mouths open, eyes wide. Idris leaned forward over his saddle horn, making it creak. He slid slowly to the right, then plopped to the ground. Blood from the bullet holes oozed out through his vest and flowed, soaked up by the dirt. The albino toppled to his left with a grunt and loud thud, sides still heaving with life seeping out in ragged breaths. Idris lay curled in the fetal position, still as a cactus plant, his black hair looked painted to his skull.

Spike felt his chest heave as he moved to the door opening to stare. His fingers trembled. He breathed quickly. Never in his wildest dreams did he think anybody might actually kill the gunfighter. He'd never forget the black's last word – 'Stupid.' He no doubt meant himself for getting caught in such a position.

The boys stared at the body.

'I want his boots,' Eddie Bartlett said, 'and his Colt.'

Spike had always admired the shiny, black holster and cartridge belt, and the fine, silver-lined Mexican saddle on the albino. He felt a stitch of pain in his side that made him scowl. 'Boys,' he said. 'When we get what we want from the black and the horse, you bury him out back far enough that nobody will ever see him again. Bury the horse too.'

A moment of silence passed, all standing, staring at the fallen Idris Harris, the only sound, the labored breathing of the albino. Spike pulled his Colt and shot the horse through his right eye. That stopped the last noise of the albino's life.

Bartlett shuffled forward and knelt to the boots on the body. He peered up at Spike. 'What's next?'

Willy and Woody began to reload.

Spike grinned. 'Next, we take care of Alex, the shotgun rider. I want that scout bastard alone and vulnerable.'

'What about the marshal, Rupert Howell? He got no deputies now. He gonna throw in with us?'

'Not likely. He'll find help. But that pot-bellied politician will follow the trail of his deputies. He ain't never going to take out Bonner, he ain't man enough,' Spike Carp said.

TWENTY-TWO

Link Bonner and Emma Fitzgerald were on the bed, fully dressed – Link with the Peacemaker gripped on his chest – Emma in her buckskin pants, her cinnamon hair tied close at her neck, her quilt purse on the floor next to her – both trying to sleep. Rupert Howell, the big-belly Yuma town marshal, hit the east side of the house just after midnight. A burning lantern crashed through the bedroom window, lighting off the dresser first then the end of the bed as liquid fire splashed across the room.

'Get a weapon in your hand, Bonner!' Howell shouted. 'I'm waiting!'

Rolling off the bed, Link fired two shots at the window. He and Emma coughed out of the room, smoke already boiling to the ceiling. Past the table at the river side wall, Link picked up a chair and pitched it through the window. He knew the crash would bring Howell around.

'Wait 'til I'm outside,' he said to Emma.

'He might not be alone.'

'I figure on that.'

As soon as Link dropped to the ground, a shadow came around the corner and fired a wild shot. Link knelt and dropped the man with a chest hit. Immediately, another peeked around and fired twice, quickly. One bullet went wild. The second chewed through Link's calf like a spear and he yanked his leg back and dropped to his elbows and knees. When the man cocked again, Emma reached through the window and shot him in the head. He jerked back and down. She sat on the window-sill and dropped to her feet beside Link, hauling her purse with her.

Flames reached the walls and crawled with smoky heat to the roof, roasting and lighting the area.

Link's leg pulsed with pain. He slid along down to the muddy river bank and turned to sit.

With her purse hanging from her shoulder, Emma came to him. 'Where?'

'Right leg, low.' He pulled up his Levi pant leg and splashed river water on the wound. 'Just a crease, ain't even bleeding much. Keep watch behind you, Em.'

Emma's lovely face showed concern, in the flickering red light of the flames in the background. Her indigo eyes looked black. The house crackled and spit and hissed as though crying as it died. 'Can't go back in there for bandages. I have ribbon in my purse but it won't be wide enough. I'll use your bandanna.'

'He'll be coming around,' Link said. He wanted her to stop fretting over him and pay attention to what was happening.

As Link untied the knot at his neck, Rupert Howell emerged around the burning corner of the house, gun in hand. 'Got both of you,' he said.

Link shoved Emma hard and rolled toward the flowing river. He had his Colt cocked. Howell fired, hitting mud between Link and Emma. Link shot Howell in the chest. Emma had rolled to her stomach, the .32 in her hand. On her elbows, she shot Howell in his protruding belly. Howell dropped his pistol, both hands clutching his stomach. Link shot him again through his nose.

*

A bucket brigade came from town to haul river water in a line and throw it on the flames. But it was too late to save the small house. Aged wood and dry weather let the flames inhale the structure the way tumbleweed tinder started a camp fire. After half-an-hour they gave up and let the house burn to the ground. The corral and buckboard were not touched. The doc patched Link's leg. A hotel room was offered but Link declined. He and Em would camp under the lean-to in the corral. It was open all around to show anyone else coming to dry-gulch them. Eventually, in the early morning before dawn, everybody left. Link and Emma managed a few hours of sleep before sunrise.

At the café breakfast table, Link and Emma listened to Alex. 'You ain't stayin' in a corral.' He had rolled the stagecoach in from Mineral City hours after the shoot-up and his young face looked sour with not enough sleep. 'The house is big enough. It's got a double bed. I can stay in the barn lean-to with Jason, where you were before Emma showed.'

'Obliged,' Link said.

'We only got four to go, right? That makes us three against four, counting Idris.'

'Emma makes it an even four.'

Alex looked at Emma with a youthful grin. He tugged the long, blond locks coming out of his bowler hat, longer due to need of a barber. 'Oh, yeah. She's a pistol all by herself.'

Emma blessed him with a smile.

'Will you be around?' Link asked.

'For at least a week. I posted an announcement, no more stagecoach or freight runs for a week due to need for inventory. Ma said to write it like that so's folks won't just forget about us.' He shoved the last of bacon and eggs in his mouth and took a sip of coffee. 'If Carp ain't here in a week, we better go look for him.'

'I *been* looking for him. I think Idris knows where he's hiding out. The outlaw has got to be healed enough by now. Next time I connect with Idris, I'll ask, so I can go get him.'

'They already got started on you. That was bold of the marshal to come at you like that.'

'Overconfident,' Emma said. 'Even with help he couldn't get out from under his own arrogance. He didn't think Link was that good.'

With a swallow of coffee, Alex chuckled, 'Or that he had such a hard-case side-kick.'

'Maybe,' she said. 'I'm not that hard.'

Link smiled at her, his hand on her slim, buckskin-covered leg. 'The woman does have her moments.'

Alex wiped his mouth with a napkin, 'Jason wants to join us. I told you he can shoot.'

Link considered the offer. The wild-boy looked very young, younger even than Alex. 'Let me think on it. I don't want any young lads I don't know hit. It ain't his fight – yours neither.'

'I made it so. You need help moving anything?'

Link sipped coffee and shook his head. 'Our horses are tied outside. We only got the buckboard. For now, we'll leave it in the corral. We ain't got nothing else, the fire ate it all.'

Alex leaned back and patted his stomach. He winked at the cute waitress. 'They might be bold and stupid enough to ride into downtown Yuma.'

'Then we'll brace them where they stand. Idris will be with 'em and hit from the side. You, me and Emma should be able to drop what's left.'

Even with clean bed-sheets, Link could not shed memories of what had happened in that bedroom with Sid shooting his wife. In the kitchen, he expected the smell of baking bread and Sue-Ellen's honeysuckle perfume and to see the loaf with butter and peach jelly on the table.

Emma watched him close, as though she knew. 'You can't escape the killing here, can you?'

Link squinted against the back and leg pain. He sat on a chair pushed away from the kitchen table, sliding his palms back and forth on his legs, breathing faster than usual, teeth gritted. 'I want it over, Em. I got to put an end to this and get us away. The reason for the killing is changed. I ain't so full of hate I once was. Do you understand? I jes' want it done.'

'Let me change the bandages,' she said. 'The doc gave me extra.' She raised his pant leg and helped him off with his vest and shirt. 'The back is bleeding through. I know you want to be out there looking for them.'

'They been hid in the desert someplace. I got a bad feeling, Em, like everybody around me – them close to me – is gonna to get killed.'

'You're not thinking straight. You need sleep. We both do.'

He grabbed her arm and pulled her close to him. 'You get shed of it, girl. Go someplace and wait for me. When it's over, we'll run off and get married then head on north.'

Emma yanked her arm free, her indigo glare smoky with anger. 'Quit talking dumb, Link. That won't happen. You're mine and I got to fight whatever attacks you, by your side. Now, that's the way of it, no twist and turn. You just end that kind of jabber, you hear? End it now.'

He sat back in surprise. 'No need to get mad.'

'Sometimes you come up with dumb notions.'

Link remained quiet while she fussed over his wounds. When she finished with his back she kissed his shoulder.

'Good job, nurse,' he said.

'Time to get you to bed.'

He allowed her to help him to the bedroom. While he wanted to ponder and plan their future, he couldn't allow himself. He wasn't sure they had a future. Both might have their lives ended in the next day or two. He had to think immediate and concentrate on the threat. If Carp and his boys rode in they would head for The Trail to Ruin Saloon, act bold, as if to say, 'Here we are, Bonner, come and get us,' knowing they had him outnumbered. Or, they might come direct to the stagecoach house-station and burn it down as Howell did the house.

He sat on the bed while Emma kneeled, her elbows on his knees. He said, 'We got to have one of us awake to keep watch.'

'I know. I'll wait and wake Alex in a couple hours.'

'They might feel confident, come at us in bright daylight.'

'Then we'll be rested and ready.'

He leaned back with his head on the pillow. Visual thinking already began to fade. 'Wake me in two hours.'

'Hush yourself up,' Emma said.

TWENTY-THREE

Spike Carp liked his new, silver-lined Mexican saddle. Riding his buckskin the eight miles from the shack to Yuma, he glanced at the latest boots on Eddie Bartlett riding next to him, and Woody's replacement Plains hat. Spike had to let out the cartridge belt to the next hole, his girth a bit more than the late Idris Harris'. Odd how slick his old Colt slipped in and out of the new holster, as if weapon and leather were made for each other. Eddie had taken more than boots; he'd helped himself to the Colt too. Other than the constant but slight pain in his side, due to the movement of the horse, Spike felt ready, his chest pulsing in anticipation.

The sun rose past high-noon and started down toward California while the horses walked easy. Woody had ridden to Yuma last night for a whiskey run – the outlaws still too hot for Gila or Colorado City – and heard the news of Marshal Rupert Howell's demise. The marshal had been dumb to hit the couple at night. An old trail-hand like Bonner expected a night attack. Once the boys took care of the shotgun rider, Bonner and his woman would be close by and next.

He heeled his mount to a gallop. The others did the same, each of the three churning in their own thoughts. Spike thought along just one streak – Alex, the shotgun rider dead before dark – Bonner dead before morning sun – the woman

136

on Spike's shack bunk before noon, reluctant and fighting against what was bound to happen.

They rode on, three miles out of Yuma.

In late afternoon, the town of Yuma sat dusty and sleepy next to the mighty canyon-carving, Colorado River. Spike and his gang rode in from southeast, across town but headed for the river. They rode in together between buildings to the main, wide, dirt road called Main, the road smoothed by horse and wagon traffic. They turned left and walked the horses past the livery and the hardware store where a man loading his buckboard stopped and stared at them. They rode by one of the smaller saloons. Two girls with tired, child-like faces watched them from upstairs whorehouse windows.

When they came to the hotel, Eddie Bartlett with his new boots and Colt, split off to the right with Willy and Woody riding behind him. Spike continued to the house-stagecoach yard ahead. A dog barked at him, its tail wagging, but quickly found a cat to chase.

Spike sweated despite a nip in the air. His chest would not stop fluttering. He slipped the rawhide loop off his Colt hammer. His gaze darted along the house, beyond to the stagecoach and wagons, out back to the barn. He drew his weapon.

A rifle shot cracked from behind the barn.

Spike galloped by the house as the door opened and Bonner stepped out, Colt in hand. Spike fired while going by, missed, turned to shoot again when Bonner shot a chunk of silver lining from the Mexican saddle.

Link pulled the hammer and fired again, right through Spike's hat.

By then Spike was past the wagons and galloped along the side of the barn. He saw Bartlett riding away. Willy, bent low over his saddle-horn followed. Willy leaned to the side of his saddle Indian-style, using it for cover as his mustang ran. A wild-looking kid with unruly, blond hair all around his shoulders, fired his Winchester at Willy, hitting the hand that gripped the saddle horn. Willy had to grapple with his right hand to keep from falling from the saddle.

The dark-looking Woody rode around the backside edge of the barn. He fired, hitting the rifle. It leaped from the kid's hand. The kid wiggled his fingers then wrung his hands together and stepped back into shadow. Alex came out of a lean-to room that connected to the back of the barn, his bowler cockeyed on the long, blond mop, six-gun in hand. He shot Woody through the left leg.

With a backward glance, Spike watched Bonner limp along the side of the barn after them, gun in hand. Bonner raised his Colt and fired three quick shots. Two zinged by; the third hit the saddle – again. The woman came out of the house dressed in tight, buckskin pants. Even the woman had a pistol.

Alex stepped into the open. He aimed at the retreating figure of Woody. His back was to Spike. As Spike rode by to follow the others to where they were to meet, he fired back over his shoulder at Bonner, hitting the side of the barn. Alex fired wild at Woody. Spike heeled his horse as he rode by and shot Alex three times, twice in the back and the third through his bowler hat. Snapping shots echoed against the barn walls. Alex stumbled two steps, dropped to his knees and fell on his face.

The woman screamed.

Spike Carp rode his buckskin at a trot past the hardware store and around to the back door of The Trail to Ruin Saloon. Eddie Bartlett, without a scratch, had already swung down from the saddle and was helping Willy from his horse.

'How bad is it?' Spike asked.

138

Willy coughed, his pink face pain-filled, green eyes squinting. He stood holding the saddle horn. 'Looks like the
shoulder. My hand hurts worse.' His good hand dropped
from the horn as he gripped his wrist. The shot hand looked
like a mangled, scarlet, vulture claw.

Spike turned to Woody who was down from the saddle and
hopping to tie the reins. 'You?' he said. 'Anywhere besides
the leg?'

'Don't think so. Hit me above the knee.'

'Let's get inside,' Spike said. 'He'll be in a foul mood and
coming for us now that his shotgun rider is done for.'

Inside the saloon, four men stood at the bar; one old
timer weaved, almost too drunk to stand. Pairs of men sat
around three tables. All watched with curiosity as Spike and
the boys came in. Once the back door had closed, the visitors
turned immediately to their left and went to an empty, back
table.

Mars, the bartender stared at them with his watery, gray
eyes. 'You boys bringing trouble? Heard some shooting out
there.'

Spike said, 'That madman killer Link Bonner is after us.
Already shot up my friends.'

Mars pulled his shotgun from under the bar and set the
barrels on the counter top. His shirt-sleeves slid up his arms,
held by black garters. 'I don't care nothing about your petty
squabbles. Anybody breaks my fancy mirror I had freighted
all the way from St Louis, gets a load of buckshot from knees
to neck. Mebbe you boys might just better take it outside.'

'Too late for that,' Spike said.

The curious had already begun to gather along boardwalks and peer from shop windows. Lanterns were lit, easy to
see through the swinging doors.

Woody had dropped his pants enough to get at the leg
wound. He untied his bandana and retied it tightly around

139

the bleeding puncture, the whole time hissing between his teeth.

Willy had his head on the table, still gripping the claw. 'God, it hurts, it hurts something awful.' He groaned then sat straight, holding his hand between his legs, pink face contorted, eyes shut tight.

Spike reached over and untied Willy's bandana for him. 'Wrap this around the hand; maybe stop some of the bleeding.' He untied his own red bandana and put it against Willy's shoulder. 'Keep this pushed hard.' He turned to Eddie Bartlett. 'Where you going?'

Bartlett had stood. 'We need a bottle and some glasses.'

Spike nodded. 'Reload, boys, we ain't got much time and it's getting dark. We got to be quick and accurate. Don't dawdle. Gun him down soon as he shows at the door.' He glanced around the room. 'You fellas in here better leave or find some corner tables.' He nodded to the swinging, batwing doors. 'Trouble is coming through that doorway and there's gonna be shooting.'

Chairs scraped as two men used the doors to leave. The four at the bar stood without moving. The old timer had his head on the counter. The others stumbled to shadowy tables along the walls, not willing to go before their bottle was empty.

Bartlett returned with a full bottle and four empty glasses. He took his time filling the glasses then looked at Spike. 'We better spread out some.'

The gang took their full glasses and each pushed to tables next to each other in a crescent-moon position opposite the bar, facing the doors. They had their reloaded Colts on the tables. Spike slugged down his rotgut whiskey, poured another, and taking the bottle, shoved off to a table close to the back door. If those around him died, he wanted a quick exit to his buckskin stallion and back to the shack. Let the scout come after him if he dared.

A piano just inside the batwing doors remained silent, nobody at the keys. The old drunk burbled incoherently with every other word either 'mule' or 'she'. Other men at the bar muttered to each other. Voices of the curious could be heard from outside along boardwalks, words low and run together, too close to make out. The saloon smelled of stale beer, tobacco smoke, man sweat odor and puke. Mars leaned back against his precious mirror within one step of the shotgun. A boy of twelve came in from the back door and stood on a chair to light the chandelier lanterns. The room lit to show more grime and smoke stains. He had no shoes. His face was dirty. When he was done, he took coins from the bar counter and scurried out the back door.

Spike Carp leaned back in his chair, his hat low, eyes locked on the batwing entry, thinking the chandelier was too bright, and smelled of fresh-lit kerosene. His Colt rested on the table. He sensed all the activity around him without conscious awareness. Who among his group would carry through? Who would fail? He felt he had no real help. He was alone, like always. His breathing came too fast for his liking. He felt a zap of fear rush across his chest. A shiver ran through him. A wild-boy with a rifle had been there. Spike did not know the wild-boy. Who else didn't he know? Bonner might not be alone. He might come through those doors with the other deputy marshal, Win Trisdale, plus the wild-boy, plus maybe even the woman. Spike Carp felt a flutter in his breath. He pushed his palms flat on the table to stop his fingers from trembling.

TWENTY-FOUR

Link knelt next to the body of Alex. His guts and chest churned with loss. A trace of gun-smoke still hung in the air.

Emma came up behind him, bubbling in tears. 'No,' she cried. 'Not the boy, not Alex.'

Link looked up to see the wild-looking boy standing with his hands folded in front. Link stood. 'You're called Jason,' he said.

The boy nodded. His blond hair stuck out around his head like tree branches. He wore bib jeans and no shirt and no shoes. 'Take me with you.'

'No, boy – no more innocents can get killed. You got to stay. You look after Alex, get him ready for burial.' He swept his arm around. 'This is yours now. If I get back, we can talk about what you'll do with it.'

'I don't care about that. I got to kill them.'

Link nodded. 'If they put me down, you go right ahead.' He took Emma's arm and started to limp toward the corral where his chestnut and Emma's young palomino waited, saddled.

Emma said, 'Link? Idris, what about Idris?'

Link stopped and looked down at her, his chest still churning. 'You saw. Carp's buckskin stallion was wearing Idris' Mexican, silver-lined saddle – and he had the gun belt.

Another had his boots. They even took his hat. Nobody could get that saddle, 'cept over Idris' dead body. They gunned him down, killed him dead for sure, and stripped him of his belongings. Wish I'd been there but I wasn't. I couldn't help. Now it's just us, girl. We got to take them down.'

'How do we do that?'

Link opened the corral gate. He stopped and looked past the stagecoach yard. Down the street was the saloon. 'They rode to the back of the saloon. I figure them inside, waiting. You ride between the buildings out back, off to the left outta sight. They'll be coming out that back door – hopefully shot up some and down in numbers. When they ride off, you give them some space and take off after them – if you can drop one or two, the better. I'll be coming along, maybe.'

'No maybe about it, Link. I'm not riding after them until I see you.'

'We got to know where they're headed, their hideout. Don't get yourself out in the open. Don't give them a clear shot. I'm real used to having you around.' He pulled her close to him and kissed her long and well.

Emma mounted her palomino and walked the young mare along beside the barn and out to cross the main road.

Link led his chestnut out of the corral and shut the gate. He felt his back and leg pain increasing.

'I can shoot a rifle good,' Jason said. 'I ain't bad with a pistol, either.'

Link looked back at the boy. 'If I don't do my job, you might mebbe need both. I'll hold you to it, boy. If we go down, it'll be up to you. Make your shots count.'

'I will,' Jason said. 'On account of Alex, this is the last day they live, no matter.'

Link mounted and walked the chestnut beside the barn, past the stagecoach yard and the house. On the main road, he saw people shut in, staring out lantern-lit windows. The road was deserted, no wagons, no horses, no people. He heard only the steady clop of the chestnut's hoofs. Lantern light came out the doorway of the saloon. When he drew up toward the batwing doors he eased the chestnut across the road from them and wiggled himself comfortable in the saddle, ignoring the calf and back pain. He reached down to pat the horse's neck. He pulled the Colt .45 Peacemaker, all six chambers filled, no empty one for safety. He would need them all.

He heeled the mare across the street. When he came to the boardwalk, he heeled hard. 'Hup, hup,' he said to urge her on. She clomped up to the boardwalk and he heeled harder. 'Hya!' He ducked as she leapt through the swinging doors.

On the right he saw the Mexican-looking Woody. He shot Woody through Idris' Plains hat and the head it sat on, and again in the chest as the jasper jerked back out of the chair. Next was Willy, his left hand a claw, his face flushed, green eyes wide and scared, right hand pointing a pistol and firing. The bullet zinged past Link's head. Link shot him in the belly then again in the side of his neck. Blood spurted in a stream as Willy went back.

By then, Eddie Bartlett had stood, taken aim with Idris' Colt and fired. Link felt a razor stab into his forehead and scrape skin and hair in a line to his left temple. He jerked toward the bar and almost fell out of the saddle. Flashing sparks and blackness flushed through his thinking. The four men at the bar hugged the brass foot rail, the old drunk spilling one of the spittoons over him. Link fired wildly. He sat straight. Bartlett shot again; hitting Link's left arm muscle. Link couldn't see. Blood had flowed into his eyes.

Carp fired once, missing Link and shattering the above bar mirror. Mars had been kneeling behind the bar. The crash of mirror-glass had him standing and reaching for the shotgun. A blasting roar tore a chair to splinters as Carp leaped for the back door. Link fired his last shot at him but missed. Bartlett quickly followed Carp out.

The door was single width; no way would the chestnut get through. Link reined up and turned the mare. 'Ha!' he urged, backing into tables. 'Ha!' Any men at the tables were now on the floor. He heeled the chestnut back out the swinging doors, ducking, and down off the boardwalk. The main road turned wavy and the vision in his left eye became obscured with flowing blood. Once on the road he turned between buildings.

He heard horses at a gallop riding away from behind the saloon.

Link walked the mare between the buildings toward the back. He slid up his left sleeve. The bullet had creased the muscle just enough to make it bleed. With the sleeve rolled tight around the slice, he pulled his kerchief and wiped his eye clean enough to see, then tied it tight around his head. The back of the buildings blurred in front of him. Beyond them, in the last of any twilight, he saw three riders – Carp and Bartlett already more than two hundred yards away. Emma was a hundred yards back, the white tail of her palomino flowing behind like a pristine pennant. He kept the mare walking. He blinked, trying to get clear vision without any wavy movement. He stared at Emma while he snapped open the small loading gate of the Colt. Pounding the walnut grip on the horn of his saddle he rotated the cylinder, letting empty shells fall out one by one. When the pistol was clear, he fingered full cartridges from his belt and fed them into the empty cylinder slots. The chestnut walked on. The loaded Colt went back in its holster with the rawhide loop over the hammer. He had his '76 Winchester in the saddle scabbard for backup.

Emma had slowed. The palomino trotted while Emma

145

looked back at Link. The gap between her and the outlaws widened. Link heeled the chestnut to a trot then a full gallop. When Emma saw him coming, she took off after the outlaws at a full run once again.

They were down to two. Every muscle and thought inside him wanted it to be over. His feelings had changed. Maybe it was better when he was hollow inside and consumed by vengeance, not crowded with feelings and plans and hopes, and love for the woman carrying his child. Nothing had better happen to her. She needed to come out of whatever was to happen still soft and smiling and filled with love for him.

Carp and Bartlett were a quarter mile away by now, and rode hard. Emma was half that distance back. Link galloped on but was still five hundred yards behind her. He paced the chestnut to keep her from wearing herself out. She was likely older than all three of the horses ahead, certainly older than the young palomino. She stretched her legs and panted, her hoofs beat a steady pound over desert sand – the only sound around.

Ever mindful of prairie dog holes and rain-dug, deep creek beds, and mounds and dips, Link found it hard to see clearly in the coming darkness. A horse might break a leg running fast across an uneven, night desert. The riders ahead were not staying on a known trail. They raced straight across raw desert land, maybe knowing their way through usage. The town of Colorado City lay off to the left – not dark enough yet to see the glow of light on the horizon.

The world wavered again for Link. His body was so full of back and leg pain he had grown used to it. A pounding headache came with his blurring vision. He blinked wind-tears from his eyes as he rode on, panting with the chestnut's strides. He wished Emma was back in town. He wished the boy Jason was riding beside him. Jason showed himself to be good with a rifle. Alex had said the boy was smart too, knew his words and numbers. But Alex was dead now. Emma had better not die.

Such thinking ricocheted through his mind as Link felt himself wearing down from the gallop. Rocking back and forth in the saddle as the horse ran, made his throat dry through constant panting. The pain in his calf seared straight to his brain and he ached. And the ride wasn't the end of it. There were still the two killers to deal with – a showdown. The years hunting, the hatred, the quest for revenge had come down to a pending gunfight, with Emma involved. Just him and Emma now, and she had nothing to do with the original vengeance. It wasn't her fight. Why was she up ahead riding after them? What if they turned on her? Rode back to shoot her down – or use her first? He had to pick up the pace. He had to catch up to her. He needed that woman in his life and he couldn't let anything happen to her.

TWENTY-FIVE

Link gained on Emma and the outlaws. The hideout had to be some kind of shack, as they'd had outside Colorado City. They had to be close to it. By the time Spike Carp and Eddie Bartlett reached it, Link had closed the gap between them. He had the white palomino tail barely in sight, and saw the faint, lantern light farther ahead. The half-moon brightened, joined by millions of stars against a clear, black sky.

The chestnut stumbled, nearly tossing him out of the saddle. He sat straight and pulled on the reins. 'Whoa, hold up there, partner.' The horse slowed to a trot, breathing hard, fast and hollow, sides heaving, some pants whistling out in a wheeze. When the chestnut stopped with her head bent, nostrils blowing sand, Link swung down from the saddle.

He held the reins and peered ahead into the darkness. No sign of the white palomino tail. The light dimmed. When the chestnut's breathing slowed some, Link pulled his canteen and poured his hat half-full. He wished he had brought some oats for her. He let her drink it all. He patted her neck. 'Easy, girl.'

He peered ahead again, squinting with his hat brim low, and saw nothing but moonlit desert. He didn't even hear the gallop of hoof beats. Then the lantern light came as a dot on the horizon. The hat felt cool against the wrapped head wound. The bandana knot was low over his right ear so the hat fit. His wavy sight came less often but the headache remained, along with the pain in his back and arm muscle, and the leg working the stirrup while he sat in the saddle..

Emma had to find cover. She couldn't ride after them right into the hideout, whatever it was. She was a bright girl. She knew that. She knew to hide and wait for him to catch up with his old horse and shot up carcass – and fully loaded Colt.

Link jumped when he heard a rifle shot ahead, deep in the darkness. A second crack from a rifle followed.

He wasn't sure if Emma carried a rifle. He didn't think her one-cinch, Texas saddle had a scabbard tied to it. Come to think of it, he knew it didn't.

He patted the chestnut's neck. 'Sorry I can't give you more rest, old girl.' He mounted, feeling the shot of pain from his calf and heeled her on ahead.

Emma had to be smart enough to find cover. She had to.

When half-an-hour had passed, he saw the palomino ahead, lying dead on her side.

'Emma!' he cried, and the name stuck in his throat.

He reined up next to the dead horse and coughed. The scene turned wavy. The still horse swirled back and forth taking desert ground with her. A trace of light perfume hung in the dark air coming to him like spring rain. He thumbed the rawhide loop off his Colt and walked the chestnut forward. His vision swung back to clear. He saw an old shack a hundred yards ahead, amongst others with dilapidated frames. A lantern shone through two windows without glass and an open doorway, from inside.

The buckskin stallion with Idris' Mexican saddle on it stood tied to a rail. Idris was probably buried someplace out from the shack – likely his big, albino stallion too. Link saw no other horse around. That meant Eddie Bartlett rode out in the dark desert somewhere ready to dry-gulch him.

Link walked the chestnut closer, head cocked to listen for any sound. He heard boots shuffling on the old shack floor. Shadows of a struggle came from the windows. At thirty yards out, he reined in the chestnut and swung down from the saddle. The outlaws were waiting for a man riding in, not somebody on foot. He tied the reins to a juniper. Bent low, he limped toward the shack, the Peacemaker in his hand, hammer cocked. He had no thought of his pain, just what lay ahead and how he would handle it. His boots crunched softly in desert sand.

Inside the shack the struggle went on. Clothing ripped. A slap brought a short cry from Emma. A fist hitting flesh with bone breaking force causing another cry.

'Won't do you no good, girlie,' Spike Carp said.

A body fell to the floor.

Link was within ten yards of the shack. Through the open door he watched Carp pick up the unconscious Emma and stretch her on a cot. He moved his hands over her body, lingering on her torn, linen blouse. She stirred and waved her arms without direction. Link had a clear shot but he wanted to get closer to be sure of his aim. Still bent, he used juniper and cactus for cover and trotted toward the door with light shining out.

Carp said, 'Gonna tie you tight 'til we finish off that man you give yourself to. Then we might take turns with you for a few days. We won't mind your busted jaw, we ain't that particular.'

Emma pushed him off. 'Not the longest day you live, cockroach.' Her speech sounded odd, like she talked with her mouth full of pebbles.

'Git your hand outta that purse,' Carp said.

Link was close enough. With the open door he could send two bullets into Carp's spine, then another through the back of his head. He wanted the outlaw's attention away from Emma. He fired a shot into the side of the shack. The crack echoed across empty sky.

Carp's buckskin stallion jumped and jerked so hard at the shot, his reins snapped the weak, wooden rail in half. The horse shook its head and galloped at full speed into the dark desert.

Link heard another horse off to his right, the running of hoofs coming fast.

Carp jumped from the cot to stand erect. When he started to turn, he screamed and spun around then stumbled toward the door, gun in hand. Emma's Bowie knife was stuck into his right eye, the exposed part of the blade and handle glinting in the lantern light. The light waved and wiggled as the lantern was swept off the table.

Carp saw Link with his good eye and fired a wild shot. Emma came up behind him bringing the swinging lantern crashing down on his head. Liquid flame splashed out the door and ran down the back of his head, neck and body. Carp danced and fired twice more, the slugs zinging toward the stars.

Eddie Bartlett rode toward Link, shouting, 'I'm the meanest, baddest *hombre* in the land! I can kill anybody and I got you, Bonner, I got you dead!'

'Not jest yet,' Link said. He fell to his left side while Bartlett fired twice, the slugs spitting desert sand by his tight-rolled sleeve. The mustang chewed up sand with its hoofs while riding up. It veered and slid when Bartlett reined tight and jumped down from the saddle. Link shot him in the side. The horse got between them. Link rose to his knees, trying to ignore Carp waving and jumping in the doorway as flames caught on the shack walls. Carp fired twice more, both slugs plowing into the mustang making it twist and start to go down.

Bartlett staggered around the horse, bouncing and jumping to get clear, and fired two more desert-digging shots. Link shot him through the mouth and again through the throat. As Bartlett jerked back and down, Link swung his Colt and shot Carp twice through the chest. Carp stopped dancing and fell back to ignite the floor of the shack. Emma, with her purse over her shoulder, bent to pull her Bowie and with it in her left hand and the .32 in her right, stepped sprightly over the body and out the doorway of the burning shack. She dropped the weapons in her purse and ran to Link.

'Are you still with me, my love?'

Link pushed to his feet. Her linen blouse was torn to her waist along with part of the chemise, but not quite enough to show everything. He pulled her close to him with his hand on the back of her head.

'I'm sorry about your mare,' was all he could think of to say.

She held him with her head on his chest. 'Just so you're still with me.' Her speech still sounded like she talked through pebbles. 'It's over, isn't it? We're done with it now. Tell me, Link, tell me we're done with the killing and back shooters and the dry-gulch outlaws.'

'It's over, girl. That busted jaw's got to be causing you some pain.'

'Nothing like what you're feeling. I'm going to take care of you now. We'll get you healed and I'll spoil you like a woman knows how. Can you walk?'

Arm in arm they stumbled away from the bodies and the burning shack and the hatred that had driven him after the Carp brothers. His sight wavered again and he held her for support. They stopped to hold each other three times before they reached the tethered chestnut. He stepped into the stirrup and swung into the saddle. Holding his arm, she pushed up behind him and pressed against his back and wrapped him tight with her arms. He patted her hand as they walked the chestnut easy for Yuma.

TWENTY-SIX

The day after Alex was buried; Yuma held a special election for Win Trisdale to take over the marshal job. Jason lived in the lean-to behind the barn while Emma and Link recovered in the main house.

The second day after Alex was buried, Marshal Win Trisdale came calling at the stagecoach station-house. Emma invited him in for coffee. They sat at the kitchen table. Win had his hat on his lap, big ears out, his wrinkled face uncertain. The marshal badge shined bigger and brighter than a deputy's.

Link limped from the bedroom and sat opposite the marshal. Emma's face was all but hidden by tight bandaging. Only her eyes, nose and mouth showed. She wore a newly-bought, blue dress without hoop or bustle. Her cinnamon hair flowed free and easy around her shoulders and down her back.

'I know it's late in the day and you folks is still recovering.'

Emma said, 'I made buttermilk biscuits. There's peach jelly on the table.'

Link had already helped himself to two biscuits heaped in butter and jelly.

'Don't mind if I do,' Win said. When one biscuit was gone

and half of another, he fixed Link with a stare. 'We got some issues to clear up, Link.'

Link leaned back in the chair. 'Talk your piece, Marshal.'

'We got the slaughter in The Trail to Ruin Saloon issue.'

'Now, Win, you know they was gunning for me. They killed Idris and back-shot Alex and run for the saloon. They was lined up waiting, firing at me as I rode in.'

'Rode your horse into the saloon, you did.'

'It give me some height.'

Win nodded and squinted at Link. 'There is the mirror.'

'Spike Carp shot the mirror before he sneaked out the back door. Mars has got to eat the cost of a new one.'

'He's upset. Even not counting the mirror, he reckons the damage to his business establishment – bullets tearing holes in the walls, chandelier lanterns shattered, spittoons spilled, comes to about two-hundred dollars.'

'Win, I ain't got no two-hundred dollars. And why me? How come I got to pay it?'

'You're the survivor.'

'Well, I ain't got it. So, is Mars gonna come gunning for me over two-hundred dollars?'

Win took a sip of coffee and sat straight in his chair. 'I may be able to help. Turns out there was a reward for them bank-robbing outlaws. The marshal of Gila City offered a thousand dollars for Spike Carp, dead or alive. Even through the charred carcass, we knew it was him. So, I got the reward for you.' He slid a check across the table to Link. 'Now, here's what I want you to do, Link. You get yourself to the bank and cash that. Next, you limp yourself on over to the saloon and hand over two-hundred dollars to Mars and tell him how sorry you are your personal business busted up his place. Will you do that?'

Link looked at the check. He glanced over to Emma and winked. 'Yes, I will.'

'And you're right,' Win said. 'Mars will have to eat the cost of that mirror.'

'It's only fittin',' Link said.

Win sighed and reached for another biscuit. 'That takes care of that business. I got something else I want to run by you.'

'Have at it, Win.'

'I asked the boy, Jason Frank, to sign on as my deputy. I'll pay him sixty dollars a month outta my two-hundred. We talked about it and he's willing. You know his background?'

'Only what Alex told us.'

'His folks was killed by Apache when he was a tyke. They sold him to missionaries who raised him to about fifteen, and taught him reading and writing. He says he was gonna be a monk, but he couldn't get the hang of turning the other cheek, so he lit out. He fell in with a gunfighter and his whore woman and learned to shoot pistol and rifle. The woman had her way with him and the gunfighter was gonna kill him on account of it, so he lit out again. He come to Yuma and hooked up with Alex and the stage line. He's eighteen. He don't take well to talk and strangers but that ain't necessary for a deputy, and it ain't necessarily a bad thing for anybody. Only the marshal's got to be a glad hand-shaking politician.'

Link leaned forward with his elbows on the table. 'What about the stage line. It belongs to Jason now.'

Win blinked. 'Ain't you and Emma gonna run it?'

Emma mumbled as best she could, 'We're moving on.'

Link said, 'I tell you, Win, that stagecoach road is a hard run, and not many ride it. We was even attacked by Apache.'

Win rubbed his chin in thought. 'I'll have Jason write Wells, Fargo, and Butterfield there in Tucson. They can buy the whole lot, the route and including all this. Jason don't want to live in this house anyways. Says it's too big and gaudy with too much stuff in it. If he could, he'd stay in the lean-to, but that ain't practical if the place is sold. I fixed it so he got himself a hotel room at nine dollars a week with a small room and bathroom stuff down the end of the hall. He says that suits him good. He can get his meals at the café, or hotel restaurant when he's feeling fancy. What do a man really need, Link, besides clothes and a place to sleep and enough money coming in to eat? I'll get him shorn and bathed and dressed like a deputy. I reckon it will all work out fine.'

'I reckon,' Link said.

Win slapped his hands on his legs. 'So, when you folks moving on?'

'In about a week. We should be healed OK for travel by then.'

Win stood. 'Come see me before you roll out.'

Two nights before they were to leave, snuggled in the double bed in darkness, Link and Emma listened to coyotes far out from town. He lay on his back to keep pressure on the wound, enjoying the scent of spring rain from her fresh bath. Emma had her head on his chest, her cinnamon hair still damp and loose around her shoulders, her bandages like a shawl about her face.

'We're not starting with much,' she said.

She wore only the chemise. He stroked her back. 'We got the new bay mustang filly for you and my chestnut mare and our saddles and the buckboard – plus seven hundred in gold coin. We're rich, girl.'

'And we're heading north?'

'We'll get to the Santa Fe Trail and take it north, then branch off to Fort Union. You got friends there – other widows, officer wives – all of you hungry for talk. You'll want them with you at our wedding. We'll winter there, and in early spring we'll hitch up the buckboard and roll on north. I figure to gold prospect up in the Dakotas. Build a Long Tom and get a pan or two. Maybe file me a claim. First thing, I got to build a solid cabin for your comfort when the child comes early summer. You can do your quilt sewing and sell them to local folks up until then.'

Emma said, 'Do you want a boy or a girl? Men usually want a namesake.'

'It don't matter. If it's a boy, I'll take him in tow. I'll teach him about the world and the ways of men and how to shoot and hunt and what to look out for from polecats of all kinds. If it's a girl, I want her to grow up exactly like you. You'll teach her your feminine ways and maybe even how to sew quilts.'

'She'll worship her daddy. That'll come easy to her.'

'She'll be as beautiful as her mama.'

'I don't look very pretty now.'

'Boy, howdy, that's sure a fact.'

She punched his chest. 'You aren't supposed to say that. You're supposed to say I'm pretty no matter what.'

'Your face is all swollen and purple, and I can't see nothin' of it 'cept your eyes and nose and mouth. Come to think on it, bring that mouth up here so I can have a taste of it.'

She moved up and gave him a good, wet kiss. She raised enough to look down at his face, her hair flowing all around his head. Her deep-indigo eyes shined with tears. 'Promise me one thing, Lincoln Bonner.'

'Name it.'

Her voice choked. 'Don't leave me again. I won't have enough heart left to come after you.'

He clutched her tight, feeling her tears on his cheek. 'Oh, my precious, darling girl, nothing is the same now as it was then – I ain't filled with hate and revenge and vengeance no more. I got myself full of nothing but love for you. My only life is with you and our child – our family. I ain't never leaving you – not until the tap on the shoulder for that final ride out of living. Even then, I'll just be waiting for you to join up. You're stuck with me and that's the way of it.'

He felt her kiss his cheek while he held her tight.

The morning was cold. Link and Emma sat on the buckboard seat, with Win Trisdale standing beside it, puffed up in his heavy, buffalo coat. Emma had the bandaging off her face but she still showed a yellow-purple tint. She wore her one dress. Off to the right stood fifteen women, bundled against the cold – all had bought quilts from Emma. They waved and said their good-byes. Two were crying.

Fifteen feet away, in front of the marshal office door stood Jason Frank, his blond hair neat to his neck, the black wool vest with the deputy badge Win Trisdale used to wear, and the pistol with the holster tied to his Levi leg. He appeared to ignore the chill. He wore Alex's bowler hat with the bullet-hole in the back.

Win gripped Link's hand. 'You're heading into cold – mebbe not a good time to be rolling north.'

'Weather is weather, Win. Folks can always dress for the elements. We got our buffalo coats and this big hide on our laps. The horses are well fed and frisky. Ain't nothin' in the back of this here buckboard 'cept Emma's Texas single-hitch and my Mexican saddle and the rein rigging – and Emma's purse. I got my '76 Winchester slid under the seat – plenty of cartridges for all our weapons. We're gonna be just fine.'

'Well, good luck to you.' Win stepped back.

Link nodded to Jason. Jason touched the brim of his bowler with his index finger, no expression on his young face.

Link waved the reins over the back of the horses. The buckboard creaked forward, wheels rolling north, carrying its three passengers – Link Bonner, Emma Fitzgerald, and their yet unborn child.